are you there?

My heart is jumping around in my chest, and I'm tensed, ready to cut and run. Alicia smiles at the man and says, "This guy here next to me, can you tell me if he's taller than I am? We've been having an argument because I think I'm taller than he is. What do you think?" Her hand tightens around mine.

The man is torn. He doesn't see a thing. I can tell this guy is worried that he's going to hurt this blind girl's feelings. But he clears his throat, and he says, "The guy there next to you? Miss . . . actually, there's no one there."

She shakes my hand like a puppy shaking a rag. "He's right here—I'm holding his hand! Who's taller, can't you tell?" Her voice is shrill, almost frantic.

The guy doesn't like being called a liar. "Miss, whoever you thought was there next to you, he's not there now. And I've got to go before the light changes." And he cuts across Fifty-seventh Street, glancing back once, shaking his head.

And now there's a new look on her face. New for Alicia. But I've seen it before. On Mom's and Dad's faces that first morning. It's the look of someone who's trying to process impossible information.

Because when something impossible happens, everything else comes unglued.

She's having trouble breathing. Then the first words. "So . . . you're, you're really—"

"Yeah," I say. "Invisible."

☾

OTHER BOOKS YOU MAY ENJOY

Dear Reader,

A lot of people know that *Frindle* was my first novel for children, but almost no one knows that *Things Not Seen* was my second novel. The first draft of *Things Not Seen* was finished in the summer of 1996, and to be fair to the editors who rejected that manuscript, my earliest attempt to tell the story of an invisible boy was all over the map. In the original story there were subplots galore. There were gangsters, car chases, airplane trips, encounters with vicious dogs, and large chunks of frantic action in at least three different parts of the country. Looking back over that draft, I think I was simply excited to have learned from *Frindle* that, yes, I actually *could* write a novel. Apparently, that feeling of discovered ability went right to my head.

After *Things Not Seen* had been roundly rejected, I got involved with writing more middle-grade novels —*The Landry News*, *The Janitor's Boy*, *The School Story*, and others—but I never really gave up on the core idea of *Things Not Seen*. I still wanted to tell a story that treated invisibility as if it were factually happening to a fairly normal fifteen-year-old kid. And the interaction between the invisible boy, Bobby, and the blind girl, Alicia, was what I found most interesting.

So in the year 2000, I again sent that flawed first man-uscript to the publishers of *Frindle*, and they again urged me to keep writing the middle-grade novels that had been so successful. I then sent the manuscript to Patti Gauch at Philomel Books, an editor I'd known for many years. Patti agreed with me that the quirky heart of the novel—the relationship between an invisible boy and a blind girl—was worth exploring. Then she warned me that there was hard work ahead. She did not lie.

Patti helped me cut away the excess plotlines, taught me to see a truer story arc, and I learned how to make events flow from the thoughts and feelings and needs of the characters, how to make a plot grow from the inside out.

The results of that intense rewriting process have been so satisfying. *Things Not Seen* was published in 2002. It was reviewed well, it sold well, and among all my other books, it is the novel that has drawn some of the most ardent letters from kids and teachers and parents. I am especially grateful that *Things Not Seen* won the very first ALA Schneider Family Book Award in 2004, an honor given to "a book that embodies an artistic expression of the disability experience for child and adolescent audiences"—which is an example of the law of unintended consequences, as well as a tribute to the strength of Alicia's character.

I want to thank each reader, and I hope to keep writing stories that are worth your time and thought.

Sincerely yours,

Andrew Clements

THiNgS
NO+
SEEN

andrew clements

PUFFIN BOOKS

PUFFIN BOOKS
An imprint of Penguin Random House LLC
375 Hudson Street
New York, New York 10014

First published in the United States of America by Philomel Books,
a division of Penguin Putnam Books for Young Readers, 2002
Published by Puffin Books, a division of Penguin Young Readers Group, 2004

THE LIBRARY OF CONGRESS HAS CATALOGED THE PHILOMEL EDITION AS FOLLOWS
Clements, Andrew, 1949–
Things not seen / Andrew Clements.
p. cm.
Summary: When fifteen-year-old Bobby wakes up and finds himself invisible,
he and his parents and his new blind friend Alicia try to find our
what caused his condition and how to reverse it.
ISBN: 0-399-23626-0 (hc)
[1. Blind—Fiction. 2. Physically handicapped—Fiction. 3. Science Fiction.]
I. Title
PZ7.C59118 Tgm 2002 [Fic]—dc21 00-06900

Puffin Books ISBN 9780142400760

Edited by Patricia Lee Gauch.

Printed in the United States of America

33 35 37 39 40 38 36 34 32

FOR REBECCA

THiNGS
NOt
SEEN

chapter 1

ABOUT ME

It's a Tuesday morning in February, and I get up as usual, and I stumble into the bathroom to take a shower in the dark. Which is my school-day method because it's sort of like an extra ten minutes of sleep.

It's after the shower. That's when it happens.

It's when I turn on the bathroom light and wipe the fog off the mirror to comb my hair. It's what I see in the mirror. It's what I don't see.

I look a second time, and then rub at the mirror again. I'm not there.

That's what I'm saying.

I'm. Not. There.

I feel kind of dizzy, so I make my way back to bed because if I'm dreaming, bed is the place, right? And I wait to wake up. But I don't because I already am.

I feel my heart pounding in my chest. My breath comes fast and my mouth is dry. I lift my head off the pillow and see my shape on the bed. It's right there, under the covers. Then I pull off the electric blanket and the sheet.

Nothing.

So I go back to the bathroom, to the big mirror. And I'm still not there. The mirror is the mirror, and it is on

the wall, and I am not there in front of it. I think I am—
I mean, I see the mirror, I see my towel wave through
the air, I see the shower curtain jump when I punch at
it. But I don't see me.

So I panic, and I wrap the towel around my waist, and
I go to tell my mom and dad.

Which is not like me. I don't tell them much. I mean,
they're okay in small doses, and they can be useful.
Them knowing what I'm up to usually makes them less
useful.

But they are smart, I give them that much, and this
looks like a problem where smarts might count, so I'm
headed for the kitchen. I know they'll both be there, because this is a work day, a school day, and on such a day
in the Phillips house, eggs and toast hit the heat at
seven-fifteen. Always.

I go down the hall to the stairs, and I stop. I'm scared
of the stairs. Normally, I have good eye-hand coordination. I don't dork out, don't drop my tray in the cafeteria, trip on the stairs, nothing like that. But there's a
problem this morning: no hands, no arms, no legs, no
feet. I feel them, but I can't see them. I hang on to the
banister and feel my way down like a three-year-old.

Then I'm in the kitchen doorway, my feet cold on the
tile floor. Dad scrambles the eggs, Mom reads the paper.
And I say, "Guys! I can't see myself!"

They glance at the door to the dining room, and Dad
says, "Well, come on in here and let's see what's the
matter."

And I say, "But that's what's the matter—I am in here!

I can't see myself! You can't see me. I can't be seen—like, I'm invisible!"

Mom looks at Dad, and she smiles that "Kids!" kind of smile that I hate, then looks back to her paper. She turns on her Voice of Authority: "Stop messing around now, Bobby. You've only got twenty minutes before your bus. Disconnect the microphone or the walkie-talkie or whatever it is you're playing with, come hang up this wet towel, and then get in here and eat. Now."

Meet Professor Mom, also known as the Director. Her motto is, When in doubt, give an order. She's used to the timid little freshmen in her literature classes at the University of Chicago. She expects "young people" to jump when she barks at them.

I've been accused. I'm "messing around," goofing off. Again. So I pull out my chair, sit on it, grab my orange juice, glug it down, and thump the glass onto the place mat.

And now I've got their attention. Completely.

Dad stops stirring eggs and stares at my empty glass. Mom leans so far forward that she spills her own juice, and it drips into her lap. She doesn't notice.

Dad says, "This is a trick, right? Do something else."

So I pick up my spoon, lick it, and hang it on my nose—a pretty good trick even when your nose looks like it's there. The spoon hangs in midair.

"Bobby?" Mom's voice is squeaky. "Bobby, stop this." Another order.

"I'm not *doing* anything, Mom. It's just happening."

The spoon drops and jangles on the floor. It's a ceramic floor in an old Victorian kitchen in Chicago in February, and I'm sitting on an oak chair wearing a damp towel. I'm freezing.

Dad turns off the heat under the eggs.

Have you ever had the science of *exactly* what happens during the process of making scrambled eggs explained to you, in great detail? I have. About ten times.

Dad stands there with the wooden spoon in one hand, frying pan in the other. The look on his face says, Perplexed Physicist at Work. I'm expecting a theory any second. And Dad delivers.

He says, "Since we can't all be dreaming this . . . we must be looking at some kind of visible light anomaly. I've read the research on this kind of thing—I mean, the research on the mathematical theories—but this . . . this is a phenomenon, an event!"

Such a useful observation. The guy can't help being Joe Physics. It's what he does. He works at FermiLab. That's one of those places where they smash atoms and then take pictures of the bits. Life is one big science experiment for Dad.

Dad's been waving the spoon around as he talks. Egg boogers are all over the place. Mom tries to talk again, but all we get is more squeaks. I'm starting to wonder when the smarts are going to kick in.

Dad gets it back under control almost right away. He mops up Mom's juice, serves up three plates, and sits down. Dad and I start to eat, but instantly he stops chewing. Dad watches as I float forkloads of rubbery eggs up to my mouth. So does Mom. And I'm watching too. It's a good show: *Bobby and His Disappearing Breakfast*, now appearing on the Big Screen of Life in the Kitchen of the Weird.

Mom's hand starts reaching for where she figures my arm will be. She's off by about a foot, so I lean forward to help out. When her hand hits flesh, she freaks, like she's grabbed a lizard or something.

"Oh, God! Oh, God! It's Bobby! It's him! He's there! He's . . . he's not . . . Oh, God, David, do something! Let's . . . let's call Dr. Weston—or someone else, a . . . a specialist."

So I'm thinking, *Oh, great. Yeah, let's call one of those Invisible Teenager Specialists. I'll get the Yellow Pages.*

But I don't say that. I say, "Mom, come on, pull it together. I'm not sick or anything. I'm okay. See, I'm eating a healthy breakfast to help build strong bodies twelve ways. Really. Mom. I'm okay."

And I reach over and pat her hand. She jumps again, but then she grabs hold of my hand with both of hers. She squeezes so hard, I can feel my bones turning to tuna salad.

She's kind of rocking back and forth in her chair, trying to get her breathing to slow down. She doesn't know where to look. Her eyes dart all over where I'm sitting, but then she focuses in on the Captive Hand—that blank space between her two hands that feels like her only child, her little baby Bobby, her life's big disappointment.

It's Dad again. He's clearing his throat. That means he knows something we don't, and he wants to be sure we're listening carefully. "Emily, now think. We can't tell a soul about this. Not one person. Not your parents, not Dr. Weston, not Margie or Louis, not anyone. Imagine what would happen if the news of this . . . whatever this is . . . if this got out into the public. We'd have every reporter and every camera in the world on our front steps in half an hour . . . and the government?—I *know* the government. They would be here ten minutes after the story broke—to take Bobby somewhere 'safe.' You think the CIA and the Joint Chiefs would be interested in this? I can tell you, without a doubt, they would. So we tell *no one*."

He stops to let that sink in.

When there's a family crisis or something bad happens, usually you get to call for outside help. When Bobby gets caught shoplifting, you call your lawyer. When Mom drops her ring down the drain, you call a plumber. Dad spills the charcoal grill onto the deck, you call the fire department. But if your kid dissolves in the shower one morning? Who do you call? No one. Dad's got it right. This has to stay in the house.

Then Dad crams some phony cheer into his voice and says, "Hey, who knows? Everything could be back to normal in half an hour. But no matter what, we tell no one. Agreed?"

Mom slowly nods her head yes, and so do I.

Dad looks in my direction and says, "And you agree too, Bobby?"

Then I realize that Dad can't see me nodding.

So I say, "Absolutely. My invisible lips are sealed."

Then I say, "But Mom's got a good point—even if we can't tell anyone, don't we have to do something?"

Dad again. "Do? Well . . . first we have to think. Things that're impossible never happen, and everything that happens has a law behind it. I mean . . . there's only cause and effect, right? We are looking at an effect, so there must be a cause. We find the cause, we reverse it, and that eliminates the effect."

Joe Physics again.

It's the look on Mom's face that makes me talk back to Dad, because she isn't buying his little science speech either.

So I say, "Yeah, that sounds great, Dad. But that still doesn't answer the question—which is, what do I *do*, like right now, like all day today, and . . . tomorrow, and maybe next week. This isn't some physics lab, Dad. This is me. Why don't you just admit that the truth is, you have no idea what I should do."

That brings Mom back to life. "Now listen here, young man."

It never fails. Whenever I screw up or mouth off, I miraculously become a young man.

Mom keeps talking. "Your father and I have always been good parents, and we're not going to stop just because of some . . . some . . . special problem. So just mind your manners and keep a civil tongue in your head. We'll do everything we can—you know that."

Dad is nodding along, and he says, "Of course we will, Bobby. Now just everyone calm down. What we need to do most of all is think carefully. There's no such thing as a problem that can't be solved or . . . or a process that can't be explained. It just takes clear thinking." And by that, of course, Dad means *his* thinking.

They're both talking loud, and yesterday I would have just shut up or said "I'm sorry" or something. But it's amazing how brave you feel when the people who have run your life for fifteen years suddenly can't see the disgusted look on your face.

I stand up so fast that my chair tips over backward with a big bang. I yank the towel from around my waist and throw it onto the table.

"Well, how about this?" I'm shouting. "How about if I just disappear for a while? You two go ahead and do all the clear thinking you want to. I'll just drop out of sight—you know, lay low a little. Then, *I'll* let *you* know what *I've* been thinking!"

I take three silent steps backward and stand near the doorway by the telephone.

Five, six, seven . . . ten seconds.

"Bobby?" Mom is on her feet, looking at where I used to be. But she can sense I'm not there. "Bobby! You stop it this instant!" Now she's panicked. She's figured out that I could be out the door and on a bus by now. She's looking every which way, wringing her hands and biting her lower lip, and then yelling. "Bobby? BOBBY!"

And Dad—Dad is just sitting, palms flat on the table, staring at the floor, shaking his head. It's the logic again. Dad sees right away that I have all the power, so he's not wasting energy.

But then come the tears. Mom slumps down in her chair and starts crying, and I can't take that. I can never take that. I have to fold.

So I say, real quietlike, "All right, all right. I'm right over here. But remember, *I'm* the one with the problem here, not you."

Because that's what they do, both of them. Like if I get in trouble at school, suddenly *they're* the ones on trial, and *they* have to figure out what *they* have to do. It's always about them.

Mom's mad, but mostly relieved. "Robert, that was just mean. It's not fair to . . . to hide that way. Promise me, promise me, Robert, that you will never do that again."

And now I'm not the "young man." Now I'm Robert. And I'm doing this to *her*.

But I promise—with my invisible fingers crossed, of course.

Then I say, "But guys, do you get what I mean? I mean like this isn't just some—phenomenon. And it's not like I've got the chicken pox or the flu or something. This is completely . . . different, and it's happening to me, and it means that I can't do anything like I did it yesterday. So that's why I'm saying . . . what do I *do*?"

And now I've got myself scared too. Because it's true.

Horribly true. Here I am, standing here with my feet cramping up on the cold floor, imagining the rest of my life as the ultimate weirdo.

I can't go anywhere. Clothes are supposed to have a body inside them, and mine is missing. I could go out naked. But that's not something sane people do anytime in Chicago, especially not in February.

School? Gone. Off the air. Not that I care much. It's the U of C lab school. It's where the professors and the local geniuses and all the rest of the university creeps send their kids. It's supposed to be so great. *Better* than Francis Parkman. *Better* than North Shore Country Day. Blah, blah, blah. Most of the time I can barely tolerate it. Except for the libraries. And jazz band.

I mean, it's not like I'm some psycho loner or anything. I've got friends, kids I eat lunch with, stuff like that. But I'm just not a private-school kid. I go there because my family moved here six years ago. Plus, my mom teaches at the university, so the tuition is cheap. Maybe my school's a great place if you're a show-off genius or a soccer god or something. But if you're me, it's just school.

But *that's* over, at least for . . . well, at least for today.

I stand there in the kitchen, naked and shivering, and I look at Mom and Dad, still sitting at the table. They're stumped. I've never seen them this way. And that might be the scariest thing of all. With parents like mine, you get used to having them tell you what to do next. But I can see they don't have a clue. Not about this.

And suddenly I think, *Why did I ever believe they had all the answers for me, anyway?*

I mean, they do know a lot of semi-interesting stuff. Mom knows politics and history and English literature inside out, and Dad's a certified brainiac, so he knows tons. And that's fine for them. But all that, that's got nothing to do with me, not right now.

So I look at them sitting there and I say, "I'll be up in my room. I've got to figure out what to do."

And it's true. *I've* got to figure it out. Because this, what's happening right now, this is about me.

chapter 2

EXPERIMENTS

A minute later I'm sitting alone on my bed. I've got my dark green robe on, so when I look down at my legs and my arms, the shapes are right. But I hold up my hand and the floppy sleeve slides down my arm, and I can't see the arm or the hand on the end of it.

I get up and turn on my desk lamp. It's a bright light, and I put my hand under it, palm down. I can feel the heat. I can't see my hand, but I do see something else. I see a very faint shadow of my hand on the green desk blotter. I start opening and closing my hand, watching the shadow of something I can't see.

I'm so into it, I don't notice my dad until he's right next to me. He says, "That's interesting," and I jump, and my hand hits the light, and the shade makes this BONG. I should have locked my door.

Dad says, "So what do you make of that? You can't see it, but it makes a shadow—except it's not a normal shadow, is it?"

I know that tone of voice. It means Dad already has the answer, and he wants me to say, "Duhhh, I don't know," so he can show me how smart he is. Again.

But I know the answer, or I think I do. So I say, "It means my eyes can't see my hand, but the light from the lamp can't go all the way through it . . . I guess."

Dad is nodding. "Bingo! When you came to the kitchen you said you were invisible, and you are. But what does that mean? You know the Stealth Bomber? The Air Force calls that plane invisible. Well, is it?"

I say, "No, not really invisible. But radar can't see the plane. So it's invisible to the radar."

Dad says, "Bingo! That plane is invisible to the radar. But does the plane make a shadow when it flies between the earth and the sun?"

"Yeah, because the plane's still there, right?"

"Bingo! And you're still here too. But you're invisible to the human eye. Now, how does that eye work?"

I'm playing along because this isn't one of Dad's usual lectures, like where he sucks all the fun out of a roller coaster by talking about g-forces and potential energy. This stuff is important to me. I may not be the greatest student, but I read all the time and I remember everything. I know a few things too.

So I replay some sixth-grade science for him. "The eye picks up light through a lens, and the light makes an image inside the eye, and that image gets sent into the brain."

"Bingo! So why can't we see this hand?" Now he's got hold of my hand at the wrist, and he's shaking it up and down under the light.

"Because the eye isn't getting an image?"

"Bingo! Because what does it need to make an image?" Dad's too excited now, so he answers his own questions. It's one of the things that stinks about living with a genius. "The eye needs light! And there isn't any

13

light bouncing off your hand and into our eyes. Look at my hand." He holds my hand next to his big hairy one, the one with the Cal Tech ring on it. "Same light, and bingo! There it is, because the light bounces off of *my* hand and into our eyes. We see one hand, but there are two shadows on the desk. How come? Because even though your hand doesn't *reflect* any light, it's not transparent. And the reason that your shadow is faint and mine isn't must be because my hand stops the light, and yours just bends it some—that's called refraction. Bingo!"

My dad needs one of those collars like they put on dogs that bark too much. Then, when he says "Bingo!" he'd get a shock.

"Now," he says, "lay your hand right on the desk." And I do, and he says, "See that? That outline? It's the shape of your hand, but there's no color, no definite form, and the desk underneath is hidden. And see how the edge seems all wavy? That's because of the refraction. Now pull your hand up slowly." And I do, and as I do, the hand shape disappears.

"Hold it there!" Dad's excited. "See that? When you get six or eight inches away from something—bingo!— you're gone. It's like our brains fill in around the shape, and you go completely invisible. We're just not wired to see nonreflective, low-refractive matter!" I feel like one of those mice in the movie they made from *Flowers for Algernon*. If I let him, Dad will think up little experiments for me all day long.

I say, "So how does all that help?"

Dad watches my robe as I go sit on the bed again. He looks puzzled. "Help?" he asks.

"Yeah, how do all these observations help me?"

"Well, I'm not sure yet, Bobby. But it's something . . . and it's pretty interesting, don't you think?"

I'm glad Dad can't see the look on my face. And I don't say anything right away because sarcasm does a bad thing to Dad's brain chemistry.

Then I say, "Well, I'm going to try to get some sleep, Dad." Which is a lot nicer than saying, "Get out! Leave my room, and take all your *interesting* little factoids and theories with you!"

So Dad says, "Okay, Bobby. Sure. That's a good idea. Rest is always a good idea."

But I don't want to rest, just be alone. When Dad's gone, I jump up and shut my door. And I lock it before I go back and flop onto my bed.

Alone isn't new for me. I spend a lot of time this way. When I'm not at school, I mostly read. That's why I like the library, the big one between Fifty-sixth and Fifty-seventh Street. It's part of the university, not the high school. I can hang out there as long as I want.

But it's not like I need to go there to find books. Our whole house is like a library, which figures since Mom's a literature freak. If she catches me looking bored, she grabs a book and shoves it in my face and says I have to read twenty pages, and then if I want to stop, I can. A lot of the time I get hooked. Like on *Lord Jim*. That was a strange one. And Hemingway. She made me read *In Our Time,* and then I read all his books. And she gave me

Catch-22 and *Cat's Cradle.* So I got hooked on Vonnegut. And I even read *Great Expectations* by Charles Dickens. High density, but good.

On my own I read stuff like Tolkien and *A Wrinkle in Time.* And Michael Crichton. And I just finished *The Odyssey.* That was a surprise. It was actually good. And I've found some good books on Dad's shelves—Richard Feynman especially. He's this very funny physicist— which are not words that usually go together.

Mostly I like books that have a world I can get into. And I guess that's because books have always been so much more interesting than my life. Until today.

After a few minutes lying down, I go over and open my desk drawer. I grab a ballpoint and write "Bobby" on the palm of my left hand. I look at the letters, and I wave my hand around in front of my face. My name is like this floating blue string.

Then I see a pack of gum. I walk to the mirror above my dresser. I unwrap a piece of Doublemint and stick it in my mouth. I open wide, and it's there on my tongue. I shut my mouth and it's gone. I chew with my mouth open, and I see the gum, moving around between my teeth like a gray caterpillar. Then I swallow the gum, just to watch what happens—all gone.

Then I work my tongue around in my mouth for about ten seconds, and I spit at the mirror. And I can't see anything on the mirror. I rub my hand over the glass, and my hand feels wet. Invisible spit. I have invisible spit.

Then I think about the gum I just swallowed. It's

gone, but of course, it's not. It's just down inside me, and like Dad said, I'm not transparent. Because if I was, I'd still be able to see the gum, right there inside me. So then the gum goes through my stomach and everything . . . and then what?

Only one way to find out.

I unlock my door and head down the hall. I'm still shaky on my feet—I've got no visual fix on my own place in space. The robe helps, but I really miss my legs and feet. And here's the bathroom report: Most people go number one or number two. I go number three and number four. The sounds and the smells are very familiar, but there's nothing to see.

So it's like this: Something like a glass of water or a bowl of Cheerios starts out normal, but after it goes through *me*, it won't reflect light. It's too weird.

I flush and then open the bathroom door, and Mom's standing there.

She blinks, and her eyes bug out as she sees my robe, and then they wander around, looking for my face. "Are you all right, Bobby?"

I say, "Yeah, fine. I usually go to the bathroom several times every day, Mom. Do I need permission now?"

She gets this hurt look on her face, and for a second I feel like I ought to give her a hug or something. But I don't. I just step around her and carefully float my green robe down the hall to my room, and I shut my door. Then I punch the lock button so she can hear it loud and clear.

I get in bed and lie back, staring at the ceiling. I close

my eyes, and it's dark. More proof that I'm not transparent. If I were, then I'd be able to see through my eyelids, right? I shiver, partly cold, partly scared.

I pull the electric blanket over me and crank it up a notch. I shut my eyes again and lie still, just trying to think, to calm down.

And I guess I do, because the next thing I know, I'm driving this dune buggy at about a hundred miles an hour across a burning desert that looks like the surface of the moon.

I sit up in bed, and I'm all sweaty, and there's a second or two when I don't know where I am or who I am, or what day it is, or anything. I'm still half in the dream, with sand hitting me in the face. There's my alarm clock, and it's 1:47, and I panic because I've overslept, like I'm late for school.

Then everything comes crashing back into my head. I jump up and go to the mirror over the dresser, and there's only my robe. And I can see some smears on the mirror—it's my spit, not invisible now. The robe's soaked with sweat, so I peel it off and pull on some boxers and jeans and a T-shirt. And socks, because I remember how cold the floor was at breakfast.

I go down the back stairs to the kitchen. "Mom? . . . Dad?"

There's no answer.

Then I see the note on the kitchen counter.

Bobby—I couldn't get a sub for my Yeats seminar, so I'm prepping now at my office. I'll be in

Adler Hall from 3:30 to 4:30, then I'll come right home. I called the office at school and said you had the flu, and Mrs. Savin will hold your home-work for me at the office. Dad will be home early, a little before 4, right after a meeting with his team. Don't worry, Bobby. Just watch TV or some-thing. Call me if there's an emergency. Everything's going to be all right.

  Love, Mom

And then a second note scribbled below that.

  Bobby—Please be careful.
  Dad

My folks. They never lose sight of the important things. Like keeping up with homework. And poetry seminars. And Dad's atom-smashing team—well, we all know how vital *that* is to everyone.

I can't believe what I'm reading: "Watch TV or some-thing"? And then, "Call me if there's an emergency"?

So let me get this straight, Mom: Your kid goes invis-ible, and that's *not* an emergency?

"Watch TV or something." That's what the note says.

So I say to myself, *Fine. But I think I'll do the "or something"* part.

chapter 3

OUT THERE

The good thing about February in Chicago is that no one thinks it's weird if you're all bundled up. When I get on the city bus headed toward campus, I'm just another person who doesn't want to freeze to death in the wind chill. The stocking cap, the turtleneck, the scarf around my face, the gloves, it all looks natural. Except maybe Dad's huge sunglasses. They make me look like Elwood from *The Blues Brothers*.

It's about a half-mile bus ride from home to the stop at Ellis and Fifty-seventh Street. Bouncing along, my heart is pounding so hard, I can hear it crinkling my eardrums. It probably isn't such a great idea to be going to the library. But I have to. I have to. I mean, what if I sit at home all day and watch TV, and then tomorrow, I wake up and I'm my regular self again? It would be like nothing happened, same old same old. So I'm going to the library to see what it's like. To be like this. At the library. As long as I get home before Dad does, no problem.

Looking out the window of the bus, I'm not sure if I'll be able to get into the library. It's the big one, the Regenstein Library. You have to show an ID at the entrance. If the person on duty wants to check my face against the picture on my lab school ID, things could get messy.

But I come here a lot, and I know the guy who's working at the security desk today. He's a college kid.

There's no line, and I hand him my card. "Hi, Walt. How's it going?"

He looks at my picture and runs the card under the scanner. He smiles and says, "Everything's good, Bobby. You out of school early today?"

I nod. "Yeah, working on a special project."

He smiles and says, "Well, don't get too smart all at once, okay?"

I start to walk toward the elevators and Walt says, "Hey . . ."

I turn back, and he grins and says, ". . . nice shades."

I know exactly where I'm going. The elevator takes me to the top floor. There's a men's room up on five, and I'm betting it's empty. It is. I shut myself into the stall against the wall and take off my clothes. I wrap everything in my coat. I look around and realize my little plan has a flaw: A public washroom does not offer a lot of places to hide a bundle of clothes. And they have to still be here when I get back.

Then I look up. The ceiling's like the one in my basement at home. It's not too high, and by standing on the toilet seat, I'm just tall enough to lift up a ceiling tile, push it to one side, and stick my bundle of stuff up there next to the light fixture. Then I pull the tile back in place.

Before I leave the washroom, I look into the mirror above the sinks. I have to make sure I don't look like I feel. Because I feel the way I am—which is totally naked.

And I hope that at least for the next little while, I really do stay invisible.

Leaving my house, riding the bus, walking through the library—when I did all that I was wearing a full set of clothes. And my eyes told my brain that everything was normal. And I had no trouble walking or seeing my hand put quarters into the slot on the bus. That's because my hand was in a glove and my feet were in my shoes.

Now I'm lost in space again, like that first trip down to the kitchen at breakfast this morning. My hands and feet don't know how to obey me.

I take it slow, feeling all dizzy and disoriented. I make myself walk back and forth through one of the periodicals sections, stepping carefully around chairs and tables. My shadow is barely there, more like a ripple, sort of like the way light bends above a hot radiator. I try to reach out and touch the corner of an Arabian newsmagazine. I miss it by about three inches on the first try. It's like that coordination test where you have to shut your eyes and put your arm out straight and touch your pointer finger to the tip of your nose. Or like getting to the bathroom in the middle of the night without turning on a light and without running into your desk. It takes practice. And after about ten minutes, I'm getting a lot better. So I take a walk around the rest of the fifth floor.

I know I've been up here on the fifth floor once or twice before, but nothing looks the same. Everything is different. Except it's not. It's me. I'm what's different.

I've never felt the carpet on the soles of my feet before, never felt the cold air rolling down off the windows along the north wall, never been even half this alert. It's like everything is under a bright light, and I'm worried that the handful of people scattered around at tables and computer terminals or reading newspapers in easy chairs can hear the pounding of my heart.

I end up back by the elevators. I'm steadier now, ready for places with more people, ready to do some serious exploring. I push the down button, then I remember—I'm not really here. The doors slide open, and nobody's inside. Still, it's probably not a good idea to get into a small room that could fill up. So I walk down the stairs to the fourth floor—slowly, hanging on to the handrail. I'm hoping that everyone is too busy to notice when the stairway door opens all by itself.

On four, students are all over the place. And I know why. Midterms. Same thing at the lab school library, I bet. But that's got nothing to do with me, not now. I'm having a little winter break. I just get to stroll through the beehive and watch the drones buzz from book to book, filling up their heads so they can dump them out into test booklets a week from now.

There's a girl using the online card catalog. She looks young, maybe a freshman. She taps on the keys, looks at the screen, frowns, shakes her head, and then taps some more. Bending over the keyboard, a long strand of brown hair keeps falling down into her eyes, and she keeps trying to hook it behind her left ear. She's having trouble with the computer.

I walk up right behind her and look over her shoulder at the screen. She keeps highlighting a book title, but she can't get the computer to go to the next screen. I know what to do. All she has to do is press F7. But she keeps hitting the escape key, and it takes her backward. I step closer, and I wait until she has the title highlighted again. It's a book called *Summerhill*. Then I lean forward, reach past her, take careful aim, and gently push the F7 key. The screen jumps ahead.

The girl does a double take. Then she gives a little shrug and pushes the print key.

I'm so pleased with my good deed that I don't think. Because if she's pushed the print button, then this girl's probably going to push something else. And she does.

The girl pushes her chair back, and one of the black plastic wheels rides right onto the big toe on my left foot.

I can't help it. I yell "Ahhh!" and push the chair forward.

The girl gives a sharp squeal and scoots her chair backward again, harder. It almost clips me a second time, but I limp over and stand near the wall—not too close, because I don't want my shape to show up as a blank space like my hand did on my desk this morning. It's hard to tell by just touching, but I think my big toenail is torn up.

Even a little squeal sounds loud in a library, and that brings four other students to see what's happening to the girl.

She can't explain. She turns bright red and says, "I guess I just scared myself."

The other kids drift away, and the girl goes to get her printout. But when she comes back, she picks up her stuff in a hurry and moves to a different workstation over by the windows.

I feel my hands shaking, and my breathing is ragged. What if I had a real injury instead of a stubbed toe? Something serious? Like if I had a broken leg, and I'm in a heap in the stairwell, and I'm losing consciousness— what then? And I don't know the answer to that.

In a few minutes the pain in my toe dies down a little, so I head for the third floor, slowly and limping a little. And I'm more careful.

I know the third floor best. It's where they keep the recordings. They've got walls of vinyl LPs and the old 78 rpm records, even wax cylinders from the first Edison talking machines. It's where they keep a collection about Chicago's music. I did a term paper on the history of jazz in Chicago when I was in eighth grade. I had special permission to use the records, and the listening rooms too. They're like recording studios. No matter how loud you turn up the sound, it doesn't leak out. I even played my trumpet along with some of the records and no one came to tell me to shut up. That was one paper I didn't mind doing.

The third floor is even busier than the fourth. I move carefully, taking my time now. I glide by on my bare feet. I look, I listen. I'm out in public, but I am completely alone. There's action all around me. People are doing things and saying things, but it's like they're in a different dimension, like they're on a stage or a screen. And me? I'm just watching, an audience of one, watching secretly. I can't talk or sneeze or clear my throat. I can't pick up a newspaper or turn the pages of a book or switch on a CD player. It's like I'm a gnat. Fly around on my own, and no one notices me, no one could care less. But if the gnat decides to fly into someone's ear? That can be dangerous.

I'm glad my big toe is throbbing. It's a good reminder that the rules have changed.

Standing here looking at a photograph of Louis Armstrong, suddenly it's clear that I've learned what there is to learn about the library today. Which is, if you have to tiptoe around, and you can't touch anything, and you can't open a book or even whisper, then what's the point?

I hike the stairs back up to the fifth floor, and I don't even have to hold on to the railing. My feet know where they are now.

At the washroom door I stop and listen. All clear. Then I'm inside the toilet stall with the door locked. The ceiling tile slides easily to one side, and I've got my clothes bundle. Then—voices, deep voices. The washroom door hisses open. It's two men. The door shuts, and their voices get louder because once inside, they stop thinking about being in the library. They talk in a language I don't know, standing side by side against the far wall. They finish, wash their hands, turn on both electric dryers, and then leave. They never stop talking.

All this time I'm holding my breath. I don't know if they looked up to see the missing ceiling tile or not, and I don't care. All I know is they're gone and I'm not busted.

Less than two minutes later I am fully wrapped and coming out of the stairwell door on the ground floor. I'm not running, but when I glance at a wall clock, I feel like I should start. It's 3:25, and my dad could already be on his way home from work. I don't feel like explaining what I've been up to.

I don't have a book bag or anything, so I pass between the thief detectors and head for the exits at a slow trot. *Can I catch a bus, or do I have to run the half mile with a bad toe to get home in time to keep my dad from throwing a fit?* That's what I'm thinking, and by the time I actually reach the doors, I'm flying.

Just then, Walt calls out from the desk behind me, "So long, Bobby."

Walt's a good guy, so I turn to give him a quick wave. Which isn't smart, because I'm moving too fast. There's a blur on my right side. It's another person headed out the same door I'm charging at.

There's no way to avoid the contact. It's a pretty solid hit, but neither of us falls down. Still, the girl's backpack drops to the floor and three cassettes go clattering onto the floor.

I'm scrambling for her stuff, and I feel like an idiot, and I'm saying, "Jeez! . . . Sorry. Are you okay? I'm really sorry. Here you go. I've got everything." I tuck the cassettes back into her bag and straighten up.

Then I notice something else I should pick up, but for two seconds I'm frozen, locked with fear. Because it's my scarf down there on the floor. I scoop it up and glance around, and I'm glad because there's nobody else really looking at me.

But the girl is. She's looking at the very place where I'm uncovered, from my nose to my chin. As scared as I am, I can't help noticing how pretty she is. It's weird how she's smiling, and she's got this strange look in her eyes. And I'm waiting for the scream, and I'm ready to take off running, and I'm thinking, *Oh, man, I'm dead!*

But the girl keeps smiling as she reaches out for the strap of her book bag. She says, "I've dropped something else—over there, maybe?"

And I look where she's pointing and I see it, about two feet away.

I put my scarf back on. Then I pick up the thing she dropped and hand it to her. And I know why my invisible face didn't make this girl scream.

Because what I hand her is a long, thin white cane.

This girl's blind.

chapter 4

MULTIPLE IMPACTS

Here, I'll get the door."

I hold the door open for the girl. It's the least I can do after slamming her into the wall.

She says, "Thanks," and smiles again, and I take a good look at her eyes. They're pale blue, but the color is strong. And now that I know she's blind, I can see that her eyes look that way, like windows with the shades pulled down. There are little white scars below both eyebrows, but nothing you'd notice, nothing to keep her from being pretty. She's a little shorter than I am, but I think maybe she's older. Her hair isn't very long, about to her chin. It's brown and straight, and it's cut on an angle so it grazes the jawline on both sides of her face.

You know how Hemingway writes? He couldn't write about this girl's face. Because he'd say something like, "It was a pretty face." And that wouldn't be enough. This face needs someone like Dickens, or maybe Tolstoy. Someone who'd take a whole page and spend some time on her eyebrows and her cheeks, or maybe notice the shape of her mouth when she's concentrating on walking with her cane.

We go down the steps, and I can see she doesn't need much help getting around. At the bottom I want to sprint for the bus, but I say, "So, are you at the university?"

She shakes her head. "No. I just come here to study sometimes. I'm still in high school."

"Yeah, me too. At the lab school."

But all I can think about now is how late I am. So I say, "Well, I'm really sorry . . . you know, that I bumped into you. I've got to go . . . so, maybe I'll see you around."

For half a second her face changes—something sharp and bitter—but right away she smiles again and says, "Sure, see you 'round."

I'm half a block away, racing the bus to the next stop, before I figure it out—the way I'd said, "I'll see you around," and the way she looked at me before she said it back. Because she can't see. Not me, not anybody. I guess I maybe hurt her feelings, or maybe she thinks I'm a jerk. But so what? "See you 'round. See you later." Everybody says stuff like that.

After sprinting, the bus feels way too hot, but my big toe is happy that I don't have to run the whole way home. The bus goes past my house and starts to slow down for the stop at the corner.

Panic. It's a pure gut reaction because there's a gray Taurus in the driveway. Our car. Dad's already home, and I'm guessing he's already running around yelling my name, already calling Mom on her cell phone, already kicking his brain up into overdrive trying to figure out what to do because his new science project is missing.

My mouth tastes like copper, and my heart starts drumming, and when I get off the bus and start running, right away I'm thinking of all the ways I can sneak into the house. Maybe I can get in, strip off my clothes, and then make up some excuse why I didn't hear him calling—like maybe I was in the bathtub with my ears underwater, or maybe I had my Walkman turned up too loud. I'm on my fifth or six lie when I remember.

New rules. There are new rules.

So I just walk up the front steps, stomp across the porch, and use my key to open the door.

Dad's there to meet me. He looks bad. He still has his coat and gloves on. His face is the color of Wonder Bread, the skin stretched tight over his cheekbones.

"Bobby! Thank God! I didn't know what to think." His voice is rough, almost hoarse, probably from yelling through the house. He's breathing hard. "I got home, and first I thought you were still asleep. And then I saw your coat was gone, but I couldn't imagine why you'd go anywhere, unless maybe things had gone back to normal and you'd gone to school or something. Scared the hell out of me! Thank God you're here!"

As he talks, I shed layers, tossing stuff onto the marble table below the big beveled mirror. Gloves, scarf, sunglasses, hat, coat. Just like at breakfast, I feel a surge of power from knowing that I can see his face, but he can't see mine.

I read his face as he talks. His eyes drinking in the *phenomenon* again. His eyes narrowing, his forehead wrinkling as he tries to see and comprehend. His mouth talks, but his eyes never stop hunting, looking for some hidden law of physics that could explain the missing head and hands that ought to be sticking out of my black turtleneck shirt.

And I see the struggle in his face. It's a battle between the physicist and the father. The father wins, and now he's angry.

"And most of all, I cannot be*lieve* you could do this, Robert! This is so completely *irresponsible*! I thought I made it very, very clear this morning that this has to be kept a *complete* secret. Don't you understand how *dangerous* it would be for you if anyone finds out about this? How can you *not* understand that?"

I don't say anything. I don't have to, so I don't.

"Well?" Dad's not so pale now. His face is getting nice and red. He takes a step closer and shouts, "Answer me, young man! What is the idea of running off like that?"

"Like what? Like what?" I shout back. "You mean like my parents ran off this morning? What did Mom say to you before you both left? Don't tell me, because I already know. She said, 'Oh, don't worry, David. Sure, that was a big shock at breakfast, but let's remember, it's only Bobby. It's probably just another one of those *phases* that Bobby goes through. Probably not fatal. I think we can leave him here alone, don't you? He'll still be alive when we get home, don't you think?' And you, you probably just nodded your head because you didn't really hear her, because you were already thinking about your meeting, your big *meeting* at the lab. So then what do my *responsible* parents do? They make sure I'm asleep and they *leave*. Because so many *other* things are *really* important."

I see the change in his face. I watch my words as they hit, piercing his eyes and ears and cheeks like porcupine quills.

As I finish, I'm so close that he's getting sprayed with invisible spit. Dad knows that my teeth must be showing, that I am as fierce as anything in any cage at the Brookfield Zoo. And that I am not in a cage, not now. I am out of the cage, and I am up close, and I am snarling.

I don't wait for his answer because I don't have to. There are new rules. I step around him. I trot up the front stairs and down the hall to my room, and I slam my door. And lock it.

And then I congratulate myself on the performance. I just want him to mind his own business.

After a big blowup, I usually read in my room for at least an hour. But I can't, not now. I'm too hungry. I didn't think to eat lunch before I went out, so I've been running all day on a few bites of eggs and a glass of juice.

I start to open my door, but then I stop. I pull off my clothes. If I have to be a spook, I'm going to get used to the feel of it. I'm going to get good at it.

I walk down the back stairs slowly. Some of the steps always squeak, and I avoid them. Alone in the kitchen, I pull out the mayo and some sliced turkey and Swiss cheese. I put everything on the counter without making a sound. Silence. That's part of what I have to learn. When I ease open a drawer and pick up a knife, the handle is hidden by my fingers. The floating blade moves where I tell it to.

The sandwich tastes fantastic, and the milk after it is even better. I start to pour a second glass when I hear Dad's voice.

I'm at the study door, then I glide into the room, my feet leaving tracks in the soft pile of the carpet. Dad has his back to me, still wearing his overcoat. He's talking to Mom.

"I know that, Em. . . . But you've got to cancel. . . . Right. . . . Yes, very upset. . . . Exactly. . . . No, not a clue, really. All we can do is be here and do whatever we can. . . . I know, but he really does need us, both of us. . . . Good. We can pick up something special on the way back, maybe some steaks. . . . Okay. I'm on my way. The north door, right? . . . See you soon."

He hangs up and walks past me out into the living room, headed for the front door. I hurry out, go the other way, through the kitchen and up the back stairs.

"Hey, Bobby?" He's calling from the front hall.

I'm outside my door. "What?" I keep some anger in my voice.

"I've got to run over and pick up Mom. Then we'll be back and we can talk, and then maybe cook up some supper together, okay?"

"Whatever."

"See you in about twenty minutes."

"Yup."

Then the front door opens and closes, and the car starts outside, and then it's quiet.

Back down in the kitchen I finish pouring my glass of milk, grab the Oreos from the pantry, and walk to the TV room. The couch is cold brown leather, so I wrap myself up in a fleece blanket before I sit down and punch the remote. It's *Gilligan's Island* on channel nine. On Gilligan's Island everything is safe and predictable. The Professor is being smart, and Gilligan is being stupid. It's so comforting. The cookies and milk have filled me up, and the fleece blanket is warm, and the couch is comfy.

I don't know why the Skipper has to talk so loud. He's practically shouting, and he's wearing a green sport coat. Because it's not the Skipper. I've been asleep for almost two hours!

"Good evening and welcome to the WGN News at Six. We have a breaking story from Juliette Connors and the WGN Chicago Road Crew, live at the scene. Juliette?"

The camera's not very steady, and my eyes are half open. The reporter is wearing a yellow parka with the hood down. She's trying not to squint into the bright lights. Her breath is a white cloud in the cold air.

Tom, I'm here in Hyde Park, where there's been a three-car accident. The driver of this Jeep Cherokee apparently did not see the red light at this busy intersection near the University of Chicago. He is in police custody, although he has not been charged at this time. This Ford Taurus was struck by the Jeep and then apparently spun

around and was hit again by a third car. As you
can see, the Taurus has been pushed up onto the
sidewalk by the force of the multiple impacts.

Ten seconds. Ten seconds ago I was asleep, arguing
with the Skipper and Mary Ann about what to have for
dinner. Now I'm sitting up, staring. At the TV. I'm having . . . a hard time . . . breathing. The reporter keeps
talking.

The driver of the third car was not hurt, but both
the driver and the passenger in the Taurus had to
be removed by ambulance. At this hour they are
reported in serious condition at Presbyterian St.
Luke's. This is Juliette Connors, and we'll be back
later in the hour with a live update from the WGN
Road Crew.

I'm having a hard time breathing because of the car.
The Ford Taurus. On the TV. It's our car.

chapter 5
WRECKAGE

The doorbell rings. So does the phone. I choose the door.

I drop the fleece blanket in the living room. Up close to the front door I can see through the edges around the frosted glass design. It's almost dark, but the porch light is on. It's two cops, a man and a woman. They're here to tell me. About the accident. About Mom and Dad.

The woman officer leans over and pushes the doorbell button again. I stand still. I'm in no condition to talk to the police. They wait, rocking on their heels the way cops do. Then the guy says, "Let's go."

Mrs. Trent from next door stops them on the sidewalk by their squad car. She wants to know what's going on. She always has to know everything that happens in the neighborhood. I can't hear what they're saying.

My chest feels like someone is squeezing the air out of me. On the way back to the TV room, I pick up the blanket. I sit down at one end of the couch. There's sweat on my face.

The phone. It's ringing again, but it sounds far away. I lean over and grab it on the fourth ring, then wait for the answering machine to stop.

"Hello?" It's still hard to breathe.

"Yes, may I ask who this is?" It's a woman's voice. There's a lot of noise and loud talking around her.

"This is Bobby." The news guy in the green sport coat is still yelling, so I punch the mute button.

"Bobby, are your parents Emily and David Phillips?"

My throat is tight. I take too long to answer.

"Bobby? Are you Bobby Phillips?"

". . . Yes. . . . Is this about the accident?"

"Yes, it is, Bobby. This is Dr. Fleming, and I'm calling from the emergency room at Presbyterian St. Luke's Hospital. Your parents were hurt in a car crash, but they're going to be all right, and you don't have to worry about them. There's nothing to be afraid of."

Nothing to be afraid of. I'm shivering, shaking. Nothing to be afraid of. The lady keeps talking.

"Your mom has a concussion and a broken nose, but she was able to talk with me, and she gave me your name and number so I could call and tell you what's happened. Your dad is already in the operating room because his left arm and his right wrist were hurt. My guess is that both your parents will be here for at least three days—probably longer for your dad. Bobby, your mother told me that you are fifteen, is that right?"

The whole room is spinning. I hang on to the phone with both hands so I won't get thrown out against the walls.

The lady is patient. "You're fifteen, is that right, Bobby?"

"Yes." The thinking is almost harder than the breathing.

"And you are there alone and you have no one over eighteen other than your parents who live there, right?"

"Yes."

"Then I want to be sure that you've got somewhere to stay for the next few days until one of your parents is well enough to come home. Or some adult could come and stay with you there. Are there any relatives or friends I should call for you? Or would you like to call someone and then get back to me here so I can have your mother approve the arrangements? In a case like this with a child at home, we have to be certain you're being cared for."

The room is still spinning, but I'm listening too. And now I have to think. Think and plan. I can't go visiting, I can't have a relative or anyone else hanging around. But Mom knows that—or at least she did before that big red Jeep beat her up.

"Could I talk to my mom?"

"No, I'm sorry, not for at least an hour or two. We need to get her comfortable. She's stable right now, but we need to be sure everything's all right. And I'm sure it is. Your mother suggested that you might call your aunt Ethel. Does that sound right to you?"

I think a second and then I say, "Yeah . . . I guess I should make a couple of calls, and then call you back, okay?" Then I say, "My dad? You said he's going to be all right too?"

"Well, he's not going to be playing any tennis for a while, but he'll be up and around, maybe even back at work in a week or two. Both your parents are very fortunate to be alive." After a quick pause she says, "So let's review, Bobby. Both your parents are here at Presbyterian St. Luke's, they're both going to be fine, and I'm Dr. Sarah Fleming, and you're going to call me back here as soon as you get something arranged with your aunt Ethel or someone else, right?"

"Yes."

"Do you have a pencil? I'll give you my number."

When I have a pen and paper she says the number.

"It's six-fifteen now, and I'll be here until midnight. Try to call me no later than eight o'clock, all right? If I'm not able to get to the phone when you call, leave a message and I'll call back." She pauses, then says, "Are you going to be okay about all this, Bobby?" Now her voice sounds more like a mom than a doctor.

The room is slowing down, and I've stopped panting. "I'm okay. Tell them that I'm fine, and tell my mom and dad that I'm sorry about . . . that they're hurt."

I put the phone down and struggle to stand up, hugging the blanket around me. I pace up and down in front of the couch a few times. Then I make myself sit down again. To think.

Aunt Ethel. I have to hand it to Mom. Even in an emergency room she knows how to put a good story together. It must be from reading all those novels. Aunt Ethel is real, but having her be my baby-sitter? That's pure fiction. Aunt Ethel lives in Miami.

And then I remember school, my school. Mom called them this morning and said I was home sick. That was the first lie.

And now I've got to pretend to have a baby-sitter. I've got to call that doctor back in an hour or so and tell some more lies. And won't she want to talk with Aunt Ethel?

And what happens if the people at school hear about the accident? Will they send somebody over to my house to make sure I'm okay?

And will the cops keep coming back?

I've got to make decisions.

The winter sun is setting and the house is almost dark. There's only the flickering light from the TV. I'm sweating invisible sweat. I'm sitting on the couch wearing nothing but a blue fleece blanket, and no one is coming home for dinner. Or bedtime. Or breakfast.

On the silent TV a beautiful happy family is sitting around the kitchen table. They're laughing and smiling as they eat. They're all in love with oatmeal.

My family's not on TV. My family's messed up. And I'm probably the most messed up of all.

I make my first decision: I've got to go see Mom and Dad. Because that's what you do if your family gets in a car wreck, right? You go and see them.

Because they're your family.

chapter 6
VISITING HOURS

The cab ride to the hospital is something I want to forget. The cabdriver didn't want to let me in his car. It was probably the sunglasses that scared him, sunglasses after dark. I had to hold up the twenty-dollar bill so he could see it before he unlocked the doors.

Turns out I should have been scared of him. The guy's probably a stunt driver for the movies, the kind they hire when they want six near-misses every fifteen seconds. I get out at the visitors entrance, glad to be alive.

Walking into a hospital isn't like walking into a library. At hospitals, people really look at you. And after dark in Chicago, the place is loaded with cops. And cops look at you extra hard.

The lady at the visitors desk has a giant hairdo, and she doesn't smile. My dark glasses bother her too.

I say, "I need to see Emily Phillips. She got here this afternoon."

The lady is chewing gum. "You're gonna be too warm in here wearing that hat and scarf, dear."

I fake a cough and point at my throat. "Bad cold."

She punches a key and then runs a long-nailed finger down her computer screen.

"Are you a relative? Because Emily Phillips is still listed as a 'recent admit.' If you're not a relative, you'll have to come back tomorrow. Five to eight-thirty P.M. And either way, you'll need permission from Dr. Fleming before you can see her."

"Oh . . . I'm not a relative. I'll have to come back." And I turn around and walk out the door.

Because I can't talk to the doctor, not now. I'm supposed to be at home asking Aunt Ethel to come baby-sit. Besides, if I did talk to the doctor, I'd have to stay covered up with my scarf and gloves. And sunglasses. Too strange.

Part of me wants to give it up, go home. When that doctor called, she said they were fine. But doctors always say that. People die in hospitals, even after the doctor tells you they're "fine." This thought gives me a chill that settles in the pit of my stomach.

Then, standing there outside the visitors entrance, I see the sign pointing to the emergency room. And it hits me: That's where the ambulance brought Mom and Dad! I start walking, then pick up the pace until I'm almost running. Because the ER must keep admittance records, right? I don't need some doctor's permission to see my folks. I just need information.

The emergency room is at the far end of the building. Two fire department ambulances have their lights flashing, and two teams of nurses and doctors are scrambling to get some rolling stretchers through the big center doors. When I walk in through a side entrance, no one even glances at me.

The smell, that hospital smell. It's much stronger here than it was in the reception lobby. It makes me want to turn around and get back in a cab. But I don't. What I need is a room number, but no one's going to give it to some kid wearing a hat and gloves and sunglasses. So I head down the hall and around a corner. It's quieter here. The rooms on either side of the hall have two beds each. White curtains hang from ceiling tracks. Some patients have them open, others have the curtains pulled around their beds.

I pass eight rooms before there's an empty one. No one sees me duck inside and close the door to room 1007. I pull the curtains around both beds. The little bathroom has no lock on the door and there's a button to push if you need help—like, maybe if you run out of toilet paper?

For the second time today I take off all my clothes and wrap them in my coat. But there's no place in this bathroom to hide them. Out in the room, I pull back the curtain on the bed farthest from the door. I use my clothes to make a shape that looks like a person lying under the thin blanket.

There's a clipboard chart with a ballpoint hanging on a hook at the end of the bed, so I write "Christopher Carter" in the space for the patient's name. That's the name of my science teacher. He smokes, and a week or two here would probably be good for him. A few check marks and initials on the chart to make it look official, and then I'm out into the hallway. I stop and look around. I want to be sure I can find my way back to room 1007.

The hospital is warmer than the library was, but the

tile floor feels cold anyway. Then, when I go back through the doorway into the emergency area, there's a blast of arctic air because the big doors are open again.

This is a bad place to be a spook—too many people, and they're moving around too fast. A noisy drunk weaving around with an ice pack over one eye, an orderly pushing a very pregnant lady in a wheelchair, a trotting nurse with a bag of blood in each hand—three close calls in the first twenty seconds. All I need is two room numbers, then I can get out of here.

There's a counter off to the side. It's staffed by two young women, one at either end. The one wearing green is using a computer, and the one in blue is talking on the phone. In the center of the counter there's a clipboard. It's a form. Time, patient name, insurer, admitting doctor, room number. I have to read upside down because clipboards are not supposed to twirl by themselves. The handwriting is rotten, but I see what I need. It's near the top of the sheet:

4:57 P.M.   *Emily Phillips   Blue Cross*
Dr. Fleming   5067

Room 5067. *Five oh six seven, five oh six seven.*

And right below is Dad's name, but no room number, just "post-op."

So I'll start with 5067. Fifth floor.

It's much colder in the stairwell, but trotting up five floors gets me warm in a hurry. I wait inside the fifth-floor door until my breathing is back under control.

Naked invisible boys are not allowed to gasp and wheeze.

The only good thing about hospitals is there are signs all over. If you can read, it's impossible to get lost. Three hallways and two right turns and I'm at the door of room 5067. Looking in the window, it's a double, and Mom's in the bed on the left. Her curtain is half drawn, just enough to be a barrier between the beds. There are bandages and stuff on her face, and it looks like she's asleep.

There's an older woman in the other bed, also sleeping. Her bed is tilted up more than Mom's. She's on her back with a pair of pale green tubes running from a clip under her nose to a panel on the wall.

Slipping inside, I get to the far side of Mom's bed. If the tube lady wakes up, she'll be able to imagine the boy she hears behind the curtain. Nothing scary about that.

Up close, Mom looks bad. There are dark bruises under both eyes, real shiners. An X made from two strips of clear tape is holding a white pad and some kind of brace on the bridge of her nose. Two butterfly bandages almost cover a small cut on her right cheek, and at the hairline above her left eyebrow there's a purple lump the size of a golf ball. I look at her hair on the paper pillowcase, and among the brown I see some gray ones. I never noticed that before. Her hands lie open on the pale blue blanket, palms up, fingers slightly curled. She has bruises on both arms. I feel as if I've been punched in the stomach.

I put my hand lightly on her shoulder. "Mom? It's me."

She stiffens and sucks in a quick breath. Her hands clench and her eyes jerk open, terrified.

I pat her shoulder. "Mom, it's all right. It's me, Bobby. I'm here. I . . . I came to see you."

She reaches for the hand on her shoulder, and I give it to her. Her head turns toward me, and I can see her eyes now. The pupils are wide and dark, scanning. "Bobby. How? . . ." Her voice is cracking.

I reach for a plastic cup on the bedstand beside her purse. "Here, have some water, Mom." She lets go of my hand, drains the cup, gives it back, and then holds her hand up until I take it again. I hear voices in the hall, but they pass the door and fade away.

She's whispering. "How did you get here? I've been going crazy with worry. Have they told you about your dad?"

"The doctor called me at home. And I just bundled up and took a cab. They didn't want to let me come see you, but I ditched my clothes downstairs and came up anyway. So, did you see Dad's arm?"

She nods, and it hurts her to move. "His left arm was a mess, but the doctor says it looks worse than it is." Her eyes fill with tears. "But what I'm most worried about is you. Bobby, we didn't mean to leave you alone. I mean, we did, but it wasn't like we were ignoring you or forgetting about you."

I squeeze her hand. "I know, Mom, I know."

Her eyes keep trying to see me. "This . . . this happening to you, Bobby, it was a shock for us just like it was for—"

No warning. The door swings wide and three people walk in, led by a short woman in a white coat who's finishing a sentence. ". . . that's the greatest concern at this point. Mrs. Phillips—good! I'm glad you're keeping yourself awake." All bright and cheery.

I drop to my knees and scoot under the high bed. From what I can see, it's two women and a man. I know the talker's voice. It's the lady who called me at home, Dr. Fleming.

Mom says, "Has there been any word about my husband?" I can hear the strain in Mom's voice. She's worried these people are going to bump into me.

The lady doctor has a kind voice. "I knew you'd want to know about Mr. Phillips, so I had one of my interns call downstairs and check. Dr. Porter?"

The man is standing near the foot of the bed. He's wearing brown shoes. It would be so easy to tie those laces together.

He shifts his weight and clears his throat. "Ahem, well, the operating room nurse said that the surgeon was very happy with the way things went. Apparently the force of the impact from the left caused a compound fracture, which means that the bone fragments—"

"Yes, that's fine, Dr. Porter." Dr. Fleming cuts him off. "All we need to know is that things went very well, and that her husband is going to be right as rain before we know it. I think you can rest now, Mrs. Phillips. If your head starts hurting again, ring the nurse and someone will come right away. In the morning we'll take another look at your nose. Now, don't worry about a thing. There's nothing to be afraid of. Is there anything else we can get for you?"

A pause, then Mom says, "What we talked about earlier, about my son, Bobby? Well, I've heard from him, and his aunt Ethel is going to be able to take care of him until I can go home."

"You've heard from him?" Dr. Fleming is annoyed. "I told everyone that you were not to be disturbed. Who brought you the message?"

Mom pauses again, but I'm probably the only one who notices it. "No one brought a message. He called me himself—my cell phone is there in my purse."

"Ahh yes." Now the doctor's voice is smiling. "The cell phone. It's impossible to be out of touch these days, isn't it? Well, I'm glad that's settled. Your son was a little shook up when I called with the news, but he snapped right out of it. Sounded like a great kid."

"He's a wonderful boy. And thank you for calling him."

"You're very welcome. You've got enough to think about without worrying about your son. Now, you get a good rest, Mrs. Phillips, and I'll see you tomorrow."

Like a drill team, three pairs of feet turn and march out the door.

I'm glad to stand up, because the way I had scrunched up my legs under there was starting to make my toe hurt. I say, "Very smooth, Mom. About Aunt Ethel."

Mom grins, and then grimaces from the pain. "It seemed like an easy way to get that issue settled. And I really do have my cell phone, so there's no excuse for you not keeping in touch with me." All the time, her eyes are searching the air for me. Her eyes get watery again and she says, "I can't get used to this. I hate not seeing your face." I haven't seen Mom all soft and weepy like this since my first trumpet recital back in Texas. She loves music. We both do. Dad listens and enjoys the sound waves, but Mom really hears the music.

She waves her hand around, a motion that includes the room, the hospital, the whole day. "It's like a bad dream, all of this."

I nod in agreement, even though she can't see me. "Tell me about it. Do you know where Dad is? I should go see him too."

Mom shakes her head. "He's in no shape for company, Bobby, probably won't even be really awake until to-morrow sometime."

Then it's like somebody flipped a switch and the old Mom is back, giving orders.

"Hand me my purse."

She opens it and digs out her billfold. She finds three twenty-dollar bills and holds them up for me. "This is all I have with me, but it should be enough until I get home—I don't think they'll keep me here long. Also, there's plenty of food in the pantry because we just got a delivery on Saturday."

Saturday. Three days ago. A million years ago.

"There should be a line of cabs down in the circle by

the front entrance. Choose the nicest taxi, Bobby, one of those big ones. And go right home, and be sure to set the alarm the minute you're there, all right?"

While she talks, I'm rolling the bills into a tight cylinder, and Mom's watching me. I close my hand around the cash, and it disappears, ready to be carried away. I open my fingers, and the money roll reappears.

Mom's eyes follow the floating dollars as she keeps talking. "I hate you being home by yourself, but there's nothing we can do about it. And tomorrow I'll have your dad call you if he can. And you can call me if there's any problem . . . or if you just want to talk, okay?"

"Yup. I'll be fine." I don't sound very sure about that, and I don't want her to worry, so right away I say, "But like Dad said, there has to be some reason this happened, something that caused it. I know we can figure it out . . . or . . . maybe we could just open a circus and get really rich."

That makes her smile, and again I remember that smiling hurts her.

"Seriously, Mom, I'm all right. And I'll call you when I get home, okay?"

She nods and holds up her right hand for me, and I take hold of it again. "Now give me a kiss, if you can find a spot that's not bruised."

And I do. And then I let go of her hand.

"See you, Mom."

"I'll be home in just a few days, Bobby."

I've got the door open now. The old woman in the other bed is wide awake. Her tubes flop around as she looks from the door to the curtain around Mom's bed and then back to the door. She's confused, and she has a right to be.

Mom is looking at the door too, leaning forward as I start to leave. "And Bobby?"

"Yeah?"

"Thanks for coming."

"Sure thing, Mom. Bye."

chapter 7
FIRST NIGHT

Working my way back to room 1007, getting into my clothes again, walking around to the front of the hospital, finding a nice big cab just like my mommy told me to, and then riding home—all that happens without a hitch. Except my toe starts throbbing again.

Coming home to an empty house. I mean, I've done it plenty of times, but tonight it's different. Alone is one thing; alone at night—all night—that's something else.

Dad has some timers rigged up, so a few lights are on. Still, the place looks like a big old funeral home.

This kid at school named Russell, his dad runs a funeral home on Kenwood. His family lives on the second and third floor of the place. At lunch one day Russell tells me they've got a big cooler down in the basement next to the room where his dad gets the bodies ready. He says sometimes they have three or four corpses in the cooler at the same time. And then Jim Weinraub says that when he slept over at Russell's once, they sneaked down to the basement in the middle of the night and looked at a dead woman.

After I heard that, I didn't eat lunch with Russell for a month. Stuff like that creeps me out.

I don't go in the front door of my house because the front porch has a light that goes on whenever anyone walks up the steps. If I go in that way, I'm almost sure Mrs. Trent would see me. She lives next door, and she sits in her big bay window all day and most of the night. She would see me, and then she would probably waddle over to tell me that the police were here earlier. Mrs. Trent is the nosiest woman on the planet, and it doesn't help that the buildings in my neighborhood are only about fifteen feet apart.

I let myself in at the driveway door on the east side of the house, the side away from Mrs. Trent. This side faces a big duplex apartment house. It's loaded with college kids. Their place is all lit up, and somebody's music system is blasting away. I wish I was going there for the night.

First, before I set the alarm system by the back door, before I turn on any other lights, before I even take off my coat and scarf, I go around and shut all the shades and curtains. If Mrs. Trent gets one good look at my empty clothes walking around the house, it'll mean the end of life as we know it.

With the alarm set and my coat and stuff dumped by the back door, it's time to eat. I'm starved again. I watch as I feel my hands throw a peanut butter and jelly sandwich together, and I think how I'd give anything for a double cheeseburger right now. Then this thought: Unless things change, my fast-food days are over. Unless someone else does the buying. Great—I can't even get a Happy Meal unless my daddy or mommy buys it for me.

Mom!

I grab the kitchen phone, and then I grab a paper towel to wipe the strawberry jelly off it.

I promised Mom I'd call when I got home.

One ring, two rings, three rings. Maybe she's already asleep. Or in the bathroom.

Four rings. It's a deep purse. Ringer's probably set on low.

Five rings. Six rings. Dead? Bad word. I mean the battery in her phone—dead battery.

Then it goes to voice mail. I try not to sound worried about her, but I am. "Mom? Mom, it's me. I got home fine, and now I'm fixing some food . . . it's about nine, I guess. So . . . say hi to Dad, and I'll call you tomorrow. Or you can call me. Bye."

I've been at home by myself plenty of times. Tons of times.

But not like this. Never with both my folks away all night. And no one else coming.

I don't like scary movies, especially the kind where people are alone in a big old house. And I've always been a little afraid of the dark. Which is not a bad way to be in this part of Chicago. Even with the cops and the university police all over, there's still plenty to worry about after sundown. The streetlights are on, but there are shadows. Lots of shadows.

So I turn on more lights. In the TV room I set up a tray table. Then I get some milk and my sandwich.

I should know better than to just turn on the tube. It's still set to WGN, and it's a movie preview, the one where Jack Nicholson is holding the ax and trying to push his face through a door. I punch the changer, and it flips to Cinemax. Some teenage vampires are having a meal.

I turn off the set, but then the house feels too quiet, and bad pictures are bouncing around in my head. All three lamps are on, but it still feels dark. So I grab the other remote and turn on the FM. The room fills up with jazz. I concentrate on the trumpet line because that's my instrument. The trumpet breaks into a high solo, and it's a bright sound, shiny and clean.

And then I remember my sandwich. I eat it, but it doesn't feel right in my mouth. It doesn't feel right when I swallow. And the milk tastes strange. Nothing feels right.

Because when fear begins to crawl, it just keeps coming.

Light is good, light is very good. But the windows behind all the curtains are dark, and behind every curtain there's a horror story, a real one. It's the real ones that come crawling at me through the night.

The alarm system is blinking. That's supposed to make me feel safe. It's blinking next to every door. The alarm system has eyes and fingers all over the house. It senses things. The system will shriek when something outside starts to come through a door or a window.

But fear doesn't need doors and windows. It works from the inside.

I hurry to the study, flipping on other lights as I go. I swivel the big computer monitor around so I can sit and not have my back toward the doorway or the big curtained window. The jazz keeps coming from the TV room, but it's a different tune now, and a saxophone starts wailing.

The computer boots up, and then I'm online and I've got a messenger window open, and I tap in Kenny Temple's screen name, Gandolf375. Kenny's a Tolkien freak, which is why we're sort of friends. So this'll be good. I can talk to Kenny online, just talk a little. Like about jazz band. Because jazz band practiced today after school. Without me.

No response. I key his name again. Nothing. I try a few other names, kids I ask about homework sometimes. Like Jeff. I can ask Jeff what I missed in biology today. Or maybe Ellen Beck. She lives over on Blackstone—practically a neighbor. She'll know. And I can ask her about English too.

Nobody's online.

Then I remember. Midterms are coming. Nobody's online.

A digit changes on the clock at the upper corner of the computer screen. It's now 9:11. I shut the box down. The hard drive whines to a stop, the screen gives a static crackle and goes dark, and it hits me that it's so early. Eight, maybe nine more hours before dawn. The lights are burning here, but darkness is all around me—in the alley, in the attic, in the basement, in every closet. The night is everywhere. Hours and hours and hours of night.

I'm sitting at the desk in the study, and I see my clothes reflected there in the dark computer screen.

If I could see my eyes there where my face should be, what would they look like right now? Would they look uneasy? More than that. Maybe haunted? Would my eyes look haunted? Were that lady's eyes open? The eyes of that dead lady down in the basement cooler at Russell's house? What did her eyes look like?

I'm running up the front stairs, flipping on lights as I go, and I get to my room and turn on the lights, and I shut the door, and I lock the door, and I sit on my bed, and I grab my pillow, and I hug it against my stomach. Because of the fear. It's cranked up. It's up past terror, past panic. I'm thinking this must be dread. Except I'm not thinking. There's no room for thinking, just feeling, feeling like the dread is oozing up through the cracks between the boards on my floor. Bubbling up through the heater grates. I can feel it rising. Like water. Like black blood. Like the fluids. Like the fluids. The fluids that Russell's dad pumps into the dead bodies down in the basement of the funeral home. The dread is filling my locked room and my mouth and my nose and my ears and my eyes and my lungs, and I'm drowning in it.

But I sit there and I don't. I don't drown. I'm breathing so fast, I feel faint. I have to yawn. But I'm getting a thought. It's a real thought, a memory. About fear. And I'm thinking it. And the thought is simple. It's simple: *nothing to fear but fear itself.* From a history class. Just words. Until now.

And then it's like I'm five feet away. And I'm looking at me, at this guy sitting on a bed. And I can see he's not under attack. There is no danger. And I can see that the fear is the thing. It's just fear.

Another memory, another thought. I'm walking out of the library about a year ago behind two college girls. And one of them says, "I am so upset, I am just *so* upset! And the thing that upsets me the most is that I'm so up*set*!" That's what she says, and I listen to this and I think, *How stupid is that? If you don't want to be so upset, just stop being upset!*

And now it's the fear. It's the same. Like being upset because you're upset. It keeps feeding itself. And then it gets you to feed it. And you just have to stop it.

I have to stop it.

I stand up and toss my pillow back onto the bed. I take deep breaths. I go over to my dresser and look in the mirror. I wonder what my hair looks like. So I grab a comb and pull it across my head, patting my hair with the other hand. Feels right. It's Bobby, the well-groomed spook. What a clear complexion he has.

Then I walk over and unlock my bedroom door, and I go downstairs. I shut off the radio, and I take my dishes from the TV room back to the kitchen, and I scoop myself a bowl of chocolate chip ice cream. I go back to the couch, and I pull the blue fleece blanket around me, and I turn on Nick at Nite. It's *I Love Lucy*, and it's funny. I start laughing, and I am eating ice cream, and I am not afraid.

Still, when I finally go upstairs, I lock my bedroom door again.

And I sleep with my lights on.
I mean, I know I can get past the fear. I just did it.
But I don't kid myself.
The bogeyman isn't really dead, not forever.
He's just not here. Not tonight.

chapter 8

MY LIFE

Wake up. Shower. Eat. Read. Talk to Mom. Watch TV. Talk to Mom. Eat. Nap. Listen to jazz. Read. Talk to Dad. Watch TV. Go online. Talk to Mom. Eat. Practice my trumpet. Worry. Watch TV. Read. Talk to Mom. Nap.

So that's Wednesday, my second thrilling day as Bobby the Missing Person. It's weird not having anybody around. It makes it so easy to think. Too easy. Because unless the tube is on or there's music playing, it's just me, thinking. Until Mom calls again. And again.

When she calls in the morning, she wants me to tell her everything I'm doing, like every second. Starting with the cab ride home from the hospital last night. And she hopes that I remembered to turn on the alarm system. And why didn't I call her, which I did, but she was too messed up to remember to turn the phone on. And have I remembered to water the plants? Because the ivy in the front hall needs a half cup of water every other day or it droops. And did I do my homework? What do I mean, I couldn't get the assignments? So if no one is online, then you just call them on the telephone. Have kids today forgotten how to use the telephone? What do I mean that I didn't want to talk to anyone last night? Am I feeling all right? Am I eating nutritious foods? I'm not just eating junk, am I? Because that's the worst thing for my complexion.

Fifteen minutes of that, and I'm ready to scream and yank the phone out of the wall. The only good thing is that she doesn't have a charger there in the hospital. I'm guessing the batteries on her cell phone give out pretty soon. But then she'll just get a regular phone put in her room. So there's no escape. I'm missing the old Mom, who would show up once or twice a day, give an order, and then get on with her busy life. Suddenly, it seems like *I'm* her life.

Dad sounds all right when he calls me about noon. And I'm glad, because I need Dad's help. I mean, like, what if the accident had messed up his head? But that clearly has not happened. Because first he explains *exactly* how he's hurt. Exactly, like he'd been the surgeon himself, or like he was awake the whole time, taking notes. Then he tells me how he's been thinking about my "situation." I can tell there's another person in the room with him because he's not being specific.

He says, "Regarding your, um, situation, Bobby, I've been running through some possible cause scenarios." Possible cause scenarios. That's vintage Dad. He says, "The second I get out of here, I'd like to run some tests at the lab. Maybe put a sliver of your fingernail under the electron microscope, maybe try to get a reading from a spectrometer, things like that. Plus, there are dozens of very fine papers in the journals of the past ten years— things about light and energy, subatomic refraction, ideas that could give us some good science as a starting point, you know, so we can generate a theory about what's going on here. Sound good?"

I say, "Yeah, I guess." But then I say, "How come we don't just do detective work? Because it could have been anything that caused this, right? Like maybe I ate a chunk of irradiated beef at the school cafeteria. Or maybe we lived too close to some big power lines down in Texas. Or maybe I inherited something from you, because you're the one who's been smashing atoms for twenty years. Shouldn't we just start looking for clues?"

Because I've been thinking too. Dad's not the only guy in the world with a brain.

Dad says, "Yeees," drawing out the word while his gears are turning, "you've got some good points there—but we have to start somewhere, and for me, that means finding a theory."

Who's surprised? With Dad, it all gets back to theory. That's what he does all day long: He theorizes. Has he ever actually even seen one of these atoms he studies year after year? No. He looks at made-up pictures of things that are invisible and comes up with theories. I don't want theories. I need some action.

I'm not saying anything, and it's too long a pause, so Dad starts talking again. "Maybe you could go online this afternoon, Bobby. You could go to the website of the journal *Science* and do some poking around, search their database for articles on light, do some reading—okay?"

I don't want to argue with an invalid, so I say, "Yeah, I'll check it out." But when we hang up, I turn on the tube and tune in to a John Wayne festival on AMC. Because a John Wayne movie is an almost perfect cure for Dad's kind of thinking. With John Wayne, it's all about action.

My big event for Wednesday is when Mrs. Trent comes to the front door about two o'clock—just as the Duke is revving up his War Wagon. The doorbell rings, and I trot to the front hall. I can tell it's her. She makes a very wide shadow on the frosted glass.

She rings a second time, and I make my voice sound kind of weak, and I call out, "Hello? Who's there?"

"Bobby? It's Mrs. Trent . . . from next door. I heard about your parents. You poor dear, are you all alone in that big old place? I saw the lights come on last night, so I thought you must be there, but I didn't see you leave for school this morning, so I've been worried about you, and I thought I would bring over some cookies."

It's the old "get your foot in the door with some cookies" trick. She really does bake amazing cookies. With Mrs. Trent, sometimes it's cookies, sometimes it's a question about how to make her VCR work, or maybe it's a piece of our junk mail that got delivered to her house. Anything'll do. And once Mrs. Trent gets into the front hall, it takes at least twenty minutes to get her out again.

I'm not sure what to say, but I guess I have to go with what Mom told the hospital, so I say, "My great-aunt Ethel is staying with me till my folks come home. She came late last night. And I'm at home because I've got the flu. And Aunt Ethel told me to come to the door because she's in the bathtub, but I shouldn't open the door . . . because of the flu . . . and because it's cold." Sounds lame to me, probably to Mrs. Trent too.

But all she says through the door is, "Well, that's fine. I just wanted to be sure you were all right, Bobby, so I'll leave the cookies here on the porch, and your aunt can fetch them inside a little later. Now, you run along and get back into bed."

"Okay. Thanks a lot, Mrs. Trent. And I talked with my mom and my dad today, and they're both doing fine."

But she's already down the steps and waddling across the brown grass on her tiny front lawn. I peek through the glass, and I can see that she put the cookies down about five feet from the door. That's because Mrs. Trent is smarter than she looks, plus she has a big nose. With the cookies that far out on the porch, Mrs. Trent can sit in her front window and get a sideways look at whoever comes out to retrieve them. She wants to have a gander at Aunt Ethel.

About ten minutes later Mrs. Trent sees the storm door swing open on our front porch. Then this short plump person with stooped shoulders wearing a long pink terry cloth robe and fuzzy blue slippers shuffles out to the cookies, bends down slowly, picks up the plate, turns around, and shuffles back to the door. Mrs. Trent doesn't get a good look at Aunt Ethel for three reasons. First, the collar on the pink robe is turned up; second, there's a bath towel wrapped around her head; and third, the real Aunt Ethel is about twelve hundred miles southeast of here.

And as a reward for my first major acting role, I have a whole plate of chocolate-chip macadamia nut cookies to myself. They're gone by the end of the third John Wayne movie.

But apart from my big performance on the front porch, Wednesday is mostly boring. But I don't get scared at all Wednesday night.

And then it's Thursday.

Wake up. Shower. Eat. Worry. Watch TV. Talk to Mom. Worry. Watch TV. Worry. Talk to Dad. Read. Worry. Eat. Worry. Read. Worry. Talk to Dad. Worry. Talk to Mom. Worry. Listen to jazz. Talk to Mom. Worry. Worry. Worry. Nap.

I even worry during my nap.

So Thursday is pretty much like Wednesday, only worse.

Besides the worry, it's worse because it's a beautiful day outside, one of those trick days near the end of February in Chicago when it feels like spring, except you know there's going to be six or eight more weeks of cold and snow and sleet. But a day like this actually makes you want to go outside and throw a Frisbee or something.

And it's worse because Mom and Dad are doing a lot better and they feel like they have to call me all the time now—which is something new for them.

And it's worse because I'm starting to see what's happening to my life.

Because it's not like I wanted this. It's not like I'm some mad scientist who planned and studied and dreamed about becoming invisible all his life, and now it's happened, so now I can use my powers to take over the world. It's not like that, not when it's really happening.

And I can just hear some guys at my school talking about this. They'd go, "Whoa! You're invisible? And you're bummed about it? Like, what's your problem? Go with the flow, dude. Check out the girls' locker room. Check out the jewelry store. Go to the bank and learn some codes, man. Go work for the CIA, you know, like James Bond, only better. Invisible. That's so *cool*!"

Because if that's what some kid is thinking, that's because it's not happening to him. He's not facing it all day and all night, what it really means. This isn't a movie where you watch it for two hours and then it ends, and then you climb into a car and you talk about how the movie was while you go to get pizza with some friends.

This isn't like that. *This is my life.*

And what's happening means that suddenly my life is completely off track. It's like a train wreck, and I'm pinned down, trapped. And it's starting to feel like this is permanent. What if I never change back to the way I was? What then? Do I have to keep it a secret forever, like a spy who can never tell his wife and kids who he really is? Hah! What wife and kids?

Right now it feels like I'm never going to get to be on my own. Like, never even get my driver's license, or go away to college. Never buy a car or get a job or have my own apartment. Never!

And how would I live?

And where? Am I going to have to stay in this house with my parents? Forever?

I'm pacing back and forth between the kitchen and the TV room, back and forth, and my whole life is on hold. I'm waiting for something to happen. I'm waiting for Mom to come home and Dad to think and Mrs. Trent to bake more cookies and the school to call and the sun to go down and the sun to come up again tomorrow. It's like my life is supposed to be playing, but the VCR is on pause and the screen is blank and maybe the whole rest of the tape is erased.

So I go down the steps from the kitchen and out the side door. That's the door away from Mrs. Trent's house. I turn off the alarm. I peel off my clothes, all of them. I take the key out of my jeans pocket, and I go outside and tuck it inside the drainpipe beside the steps.

And I go around the front corner of the house and walk west, right past Mrs. Trent's window. The weatherman said it was going to be unseasonably warm, and for once it was the truth.

It's about 65 degrees, so it feels like when the air conditioner is up on high. I can bear it, so I'm going for a walk. Today. Right now. In the sunshine. Because I can. Because I want to. Because I'm not going to just sit around and wait for stuff to happen anymore. I'm still me, and I have a life. It's a weird life, but it's still mine.

It's still mine.

chapter 9

LONE WARRIOR

Last year our world history teacher told us how the ancient Greeks used to go into battle naked. Fighting with swords and shields and spears. Naked. And how they used to hold their athletic contests naked. Running and wrestling and throwing the discus. Naked.

Tough guys.

Tougher than I am.

Walking west toward the university, I miss my clothes. And not just the warmth, not just because it's only about 65 and the breeze is picking up. I miss the feeling of protection.

But I think that maybe I get what the Greeks were up to. Because being naked outside, out here on the battlefield, it's like I've never been this charged up, this alert, this ready for anything. There's no chance I'm going to make a mistake, because I've got no armor. There's only this thin layer of naked skin holding my life inside it, so am I going to let a sword or a spear or some kid on a skateboard take me out? No way.

And if I have to run a marathon or jump onto a brick wall to get out of the way of some girl in spandex on a mountain bike, why should I carry a single ounce of extra weight?

Those Greek generals weren't stupid. Want your warriors and runners to be fast? Want 'em to fight like crazy and be extra careful and completely awake all the time? All you have to do is take away their clothes.

Yeah, so I'm thinking deep thoughts. But mostly I'm having fun. Because after three days of building a prison around my head, I'm out on the town. I'm a free man. Me and John Wayne, we're men of action.

In real life, no one looks at anyone else very long. I can always tell if someone is looking at me. Most people can, I think. Because when someone does look at you, and you notice it, you look back at them, and they look away, right? Especially strangers. I could never be on one of those reality TV shows where a camera keeps staring and staring, watching everything I do.

But today I can stare at people as long as I want to. Bobby, the Human Hidden Camera. Up close and personal.

Like this guy who's walking the same direction I am. He's about eighteen, and he's got on baggy blue jeans and a snowboard sweater and a beanie, and I'm watching him. When some other kids come toward us, he gets this look on his face, very cool, very into his own head. He swings his shoulders, and he bobs his chin up and down. When the kids are past us, the dudewalk stops, switched off. Then the kid scratches his head, picks his nose, wipes the booger onto his jeans, and takes a kick at a pigeon on the sidewalk. Because no one is looking. Except a lone Greek warrior.

I feel like I'm hurrying, and then I know why. In the back of my mind I've known since the second I left my house. It's because I'm at Fifty-ninth and Kenwood, and the timer in my head tells me that classes at the lab school are just about over for the day and, if I hurry, I can go stand out front and see what's happening.

Turns out it's a fairly dangerous idea, because I'm in front of the entrance at dismissal, and there's no place to keep out of the way. Four doors are draining straight at me with about three hundred kids streaming down the steps and across the lawns, headed for the cars and buses and sidewalks that take them home. Three days ago I was right in the middle of the herd. It's hard enough to keep from getting trampled when everyone can actually see you, so I scramble to one side and use a bike rack as a safety zone. I lean backward, but only for a second. The metal bars feel like icicles against the backs of my thighs.

I spot Kenny Temple, and I smile because I know he's saying something funny. He's always funny. He's talking with Jay Bender, and they're laughing and shoving each other. Kenny's got his backpack over one shoulder and his jacket's open, flapping. He's got his sax case in his right hand, and that big red book in his left hand. It's the fiftieth-anniversary edition of *The Lord of the Rings*. Kenny hasn't let it out of his sight since he got it for his birthday three weeks ago. The best part is that the book comes with a full set of maps.

Then Kenny's onto his bus, and the kids keep coming. A gang of sophomore girls, the popular ones. Maya, Leslie, Carol, Jessica, and three or four others whose names I've never learned. Because what would be the point of that? I know Jessica from my honors biology class. But she doesn't know me.

The girls glide down the front steps like a unit, like airplanes in formation. Jessica's the wing leader, tossing her head, lips curled in a smile. The others take their cues from her. Jessica's talking, and the squadron is listening. They're listening like Jessica is telling them the secrets of the universe, those funny, clever, precious secrets, the secrets that make them the chosen ones. And I'm not the only guy—or girl—looking at them. And they know it.

But I turn away. Because I am a Greek warrior, and they are beneath my notice.

My eyes are pulled back to the steps. Right behind the girls come the soccer gods. In Texas it was the football. At the lab school it's the soccer. Season's been over for months, but not the swaggering. That lasts all year. I could easily step out and trip Josh Ackerly, see him stumble and sprawl down the steps. But why should a great warrior stoop to even notice such a pathetic creature? Besides, watching Josh fall might make me laugh out loud, and I have taken a vow of silence.

The traffic thins, and a few teachers mill around the doors. Dr. Lane. Mrs. Berg. Mr. Kaplan. And then the buses pull away, and the flow trickles down to a few stragglers.

Show's over. School's out.

I've been standing still too long. Now the warrior is cold. I'm tempted to go inside and warm up, but I know I wouldn't feel comfortable in there. Still, it would be fun to find Mr. Stojis, maybe do a little floating trumpet act for him down in the band room, see if he wants to work it into the program for the spring jazz concert.

But Mr. Stojis will have to wait. I have other things to do. Like keep my feet from freezing out here on the battlefield. If I go a few more blocks, I can relax in a place where I always feel at home, a place with no gray linoleum on the floor, a place that won't smell like cafeteria food.

So I double-time it toward the big university library. I need to walk on warm carpet for a while. If the ancient Greeks had lived next to Lake Michigan instead of the Mediterranean Sea, maybe they'd have reconsidered the nakedness thing.

Walt's at the check-in desk again, but he has no authority over me today. Warriors don't ask permission. I march past his guard post, hidden behind my shield.

Warmth. Heat is a good thing. Cold makes it impossible to relax. Cold plus naked is even worse. But this, this is nice. Cozy and bright. And clean, soft carpets. No broken glass to step around, no dog poop, no half-melted slush.

I burst into the stairwell, and I feel like I'm flying, running up the stairs two at a time. It's like this body I can't see weighs nothing. And I know where I'm going. To the third floor. The perfect place, a little fortress where a soldier can get some R & R. I'm headed for one of those soundproof listening rooms. I should be able to smuggle a good CD into one of those rooms somehow. How tough could it be? A CD isn't that big, right?

Maybe hide one under my arm? Then I can block the door and settle into a big soft chair and listen to Miles Davis while my feet thaw out. There are four rooms. All I need is one.

There's a study group in the first listening room, five serious people, grim. I'm thinking they're in law school, maybe pre-med. In the second room a guy holding an orchestra baton is facing the wall opposite the door. He's on his feet, swaying with the music, conducting with all his might. Two people are pacing around in the third room, a man and a woman practicing a theater scene. Very dramatic.

The last room is being used too. But it's just one person, and she's only using a laptop. I feel like pounding on the door and yelling, "Hey, this is a *listening* room, sister. You can tap on that thing anywhere, so beat it!"And I'm about to turn away when I recognize her.

And I pause, and I gulp, and I tap on the door softly and then step inside the room quickly and shut the door behind me.

Because I know this girl, and I'm feeling brave right now. Brave enough to break my vow of silence.

That's because the girl tapping on the laptop is the girl I met on Tuesday. It's the blind girl.

chapter 10

PUSH AND PULL

The girl is startled, and so am I. Because she's not just typing on her laptop. I didn't see the slim tape recorder on the table next to her computer, and a man's voice is speaking:

. . . he had almost gone by before Hester Prynne could gather voice enough to attract his observation. At length, she succeeded.

"Arthur Dimmesdale!" she said, faintly at first; then louder, but hoarsely. "Arthur Dimmesdale!"

I know those names. She's listening to an audiobook. She's reading.

My hand is still on the doorknob. She's turned toward me in her chair, her face a mix of curiosity and concern.

I could still back out. I could turn around and go silently out of the room and she'd never know it was me.

But it's been three days since I've talked to anyone except Mom and Dad. And Mrs. Trent and Dr. Fleming. And a couple of cabdrivers. So basically, it's been three days with no human contact.

She says, "Hello? . . ." And it strikes me that she's easily the prettiest girl who's said hello to me in at least two years.

So I try to sound normal—as normal as a naked guy can sound—and I say, "Hi, I'm . . . I'm sorry to barge in, but I saw you, and . . . and I wanted to say hi." Her head tilts a little to one side, and her hair falls away from one cheek. "You don't really know me, but I'm the guy—"

She nods, smiling a little. "The guy who ran into me down by the entrance on Tuesday, right? I remember your voice. You made a strong first impression." Bigger smile now. A sense of humor.

"Yeah, I'm really sorry about that . . . and that I had to run off too, but I was late for something."

She shrugs, still smiling. "No big deal. I'm usually the one who bumps into things. It was a nice change."

I don't know what else to say, and neither does she. The tape recorder is still talking, like a third person trying to keep the conversation alive. I notice her hands, long fingers, sensitive, never completely still. As if she can tell I'm looking at her hands, she stirs, feels around a little, pushes a button, and the voice stops.

In the quiet I say, "*The Scarlet Letter*, right? We read that first semester. How do you like it?"

She wrinkles her nose and shakes her head. "Too slow for me. I like books with more action."

"Yeah, me too."

And we're stuck again. I'm starting to wish I hadn't opened her door. "So, do you come and study here a lot?"

She nods. "I've got this room reserved four times a week. I live pretty close. A couple hours here is better than being stranded at home all the time."

"So you don't really go to school, like not every day?"

"Like never. I take correspondence courses. Independent study."

"Through the U of C? So you can use the library and stuff?"

She shakes her head again. "I've got an ID because my dad teaches here. I take courses from a special school up on the North Shore."

"Your dad teaches here? So does my mom." Something safe to talk about. Lame, but safe. "She's into English literature. What's your dad teach?"

"Astronomy mostly, and some math." She does the nose wrinkle again. "He's pretty much of a nerd."

So we could also talk about our dads, try to figure out which one is nerdier. Except before I stop to think, I hear myself asking, "How long have you been blind?" Right away her smile freezes and she gets this half-confused look on her face, and she starts to turn red. I can't tell if she's mad or embarrassed. So I try to back off. "I mean, like I'm not trying to get personal, but I just wondered . . . because I really don't know anyone who's blind, and I was just—"

"Curious?" she says, and her right eyebrow lifts up. "You were curious about the little blind girl?" There's an edge to her voice. Not angry exactly. More like sarcastic and a little amused, like she can tell I'm embarrassed now, so she's messing with me. "It's all right," she says. "I can talk about it. I've only been blind for about two years."

"Was it an accident or something?"

"An accident? An accident, you mean, like as opposed to maybe I made myself blind on purpose, maybe by poking myself with a sharp pencil? Or, like a pot of acid blew up in science class—that kind of accident? Is that what you mean?" Definitely sarcastic now.

I put my hands up like I'm backing off. Which is stupid twice—first, because I'm invisible, and second, because even if I wasn't, she's blind. But I put my hands up anyway and say, "Hey. It's okay. You don't want to talk, I'll just go away. Really. Didn't mean to bother, didn't mean to take you away from your wonderful novel." Sarcasm is a lot more fun to give than receive.

Then I say, "So long," and I turn and open the door, and I'm gone, pulling the door shut with a thump. Because who needs this? And besides, my feet aren't cold anymore.

I'm about five steps away when her door opens behind me, and she says, "Hey . . . can you come back?"

Six or seven students turn to look, some sitting at terminals and some studying at tables by the windows. They're trying to figure out who the girl's talking to. I walk back quickly, and when I'm close, I use a library whisper and I say, "Okay."

She turns and sits down at the table again. I shut the door and take a look at our audience of students. They don't have time to worry about some girl who calls out to no one and then closes her door again. Midterms are coming. They go back to work.

I'd like to sit down, but I'm not sure I want to plant my bare bottom on some public piece of university property. I solve the problem by pulling out a chair, folding my right leg onto it, and then sitting on my leg.

When she hears me sit down, she aims a sheepish smile my way and says, "Sorry. I didn't mean to—"

"No," I say, "really, it's my fault. I didn't mean to be nosy. You don't even know me. I shouldn't have asked that. I . . . I've been on my own a lot for the last couple of days, so I've been doing a lot of thinking, and it's like I've forgotten how to talk to people. So when I thought that question, I just kind of said it right out loud. I mean, like, a week ago, I probably wouldn't have even said hi. So you've got nothing to be sorry about."

There are so many different kinds of smiles. This one she smiles at me is a new one. It's warm, but there's tons of other stuff behind it. Like sadness. And loneliness. A lot of loneliness, I think.

And she says, "What do you mean, about being on your own a lot?"

I start carefully. "You know on Tuesday, like, a couple of hours after I ran into you at the library? My parents got in a car wreck, and they're going to be okay, but they're still in the hospital."

She's got a great face, the kind where what she's feeling is right there. And it's okay to just keep staring at her, because she can't see me—I mean, like even if I could be seen. But it's not like watching that guy on the street, because this girl knows I'm here. She knows I exist. And she must know I'm looking at her face. It's a face worth memorizing.

Her eyebrows come together. "And you're staying at home by yourself? Your parents said that was okay?"

"Yeah. It's sort of complicated, but that's the way it's been."

"So you just take a bus to school?"

"I've been at home."

"Sick?"

"Not really, just not ready to face school right now." I'm ready to stop talking about me. "So, do you like the correspondence course thing? Sounds pretty nice, I mean, not going to school and all."

She gives this funny little snort. "The only reason it sounds good is because you're not locked into it. I don't have any choice." She pauses, then decides to keep talking. "I called you back because no one ever asks me about being blind or how it happened or anything. Most people just try to avoid me, especially other kids. It's like they pretend not to notice. So when you asked that, it was a surprise. And it doesn't take much to get me feeling sorry for myself—it happens in a second. And then I get mad."

"And don't forget sarcastic."

She grins and almost laughs. "Right. And sarcastic."

A beeping sound fills the small room, coming from the laptop. Then this demented-sounding voice says, "Three-fifty-five P.M."

She smiles. "That's Albert. He lives in my computer. I've got to be out of here in five minutes." She pauses again, thoughts running across her face. Then, "Are you going home soon? Because I've got to head home, but if you're going to leave soon, we could walk a little. It's a pretty nice day outside."

So I say, "Sure, let's go."

In two minutes her laptop and tape player are packed away. She puts on her coat and backpack and picks up her long white cane.

And we're on the move.

chapter 11

CLOSE CALLS

Frst comes the elevator test. We get on at the third floor of the library with two other people, and then four more students with enormous backpacks pile in at the second floor. It could get very bad—people crushing my feet, shoving me into the walls, discovering the alien in their midst, screaming, freaking out.

But none of that happens. Everyone jams onto the far side of the elevator, and no one says a word. And I can see it's because this girl's long white cane is like a magic wand. She holds it in front of her, almost vertical to take up less room, her fingers on it like it's a long pencil, and it comes up almost to her nose. No one wants to bump into the blind girl. So her cane is why I pass the elevator test so easily. Plus, it's a short ride to the first floor.

We go past security, and there's Walt. He sees the girl and says, "Hey, Alicia. How's it goin'?"

She smiles and says, "Fine. See you tomorrow." We don't slow down. And now I know her name. Alicia.

I feel awkward. I don't know if I should offer to guide her or what. She holds her cane out ahead of her, sweeping it back and forth like radar. When it touches the door, she stops.

Softly, I say, "I'll get that," and she waits while I push

it open, and then she's off again, out and down the steps to the pavement.

I know she must have traveled this route a lot of times, but the way she steps ahead is still pretty amazing. So I say, "You get around by yourself really well."

She gives me a thin smile and says, "Yeah, and if I work extra hard for another ten years or so, I'll be able to go places about as easily as your average six-year-old on crutches. So *that's* something to look forward to, right?" Then her smile warms up. "Oops. More sarcasm."

We're facing the street in front of the library entrance. She stops and brings the cane straight up in front of her. She points west and says, "I live about four blocks that way. How about you?" And she smiles. I'm not a hundred percent sure, but I think she'd like to keep talking.

I start carefully. "I live south and east of here . . . but I could take a little detour. Four blocks isn't so far." Which isn't exactly true. It's at least five degrees colder now, and the breeze has shifted. It's coming in off the lake. I'm cold, but I have shifted back to Greek warrior mode. What's a little discomfort to one such as I?

She says, "That's great," then she puts out her right hand toward me. "Here, let me hold on to your elbow. That way we can walk closer to your speed instead of mine. You can be my eyes for a few blocks, okay?"

Okay? No. It's not okay. You see, I've got no clothes on, and you're a girl who wants to hold my arm and go for a stroll along Fifty-seventh Street.

But I can't say that. If I say "No, thanks," then it'll be

like I think she's a leper or something, and it'll hurt her feelings—which seems easy to do.

So I take half a step closer, and I stick out my elbow and bring it to her hand, which is not so easy when you can't see your own arm. She takes hold lightly, and we start walking west. I have to shorten my stride because I'm taller.

I'd like to just walk along and talk with her, but there are other people on the sidewalks, too much else to deal with. But when we get away from the library, there are fewer people, and there's also traffic noise, so I'm not afraid to talk. Plus, she's right about people avoiding her. No one walks near her, no one even looks at her for more than a second.

"So I heard Walt call you Alicia back there. Nice name."

She says, "Thanks. What's yours?"

"Bobby. Bobby Phillips."

I stink at small talk. We walk along, just walking, and that's fine because a guy and a girl come up right behind us, and then they split and go past on either side of us when we're almost to Ellis Avenue. The guy is on my side, and I'm ready to dodge him if he starts to plow into my space, but he sees Alicia's white cane and makes a wide arc to my right. Saved again by the magic wand.

Then I say, "So, if you're doing this walk alone, you're listening to the traffic, right? To tell when the lights have changed?"

She nods. "Yeah, and the sounds let me know how close I'm getting to the corner too. That helps if you have to be ready for a step down. But I know this route really well, and all the curbs have wheelchair cuts. Those are good for me too."

And then we're at the corner, and the light has changed, and we're halfway across the street.

Then, trouble.

Whipping up the opposite sidewalk from behind the parked cars, it's a boy, and he's kicking along on a little silver scooter. He's about twelve, and he's got some control problems with the thing, and he's got his head down and he can't see us because his helmet has a visor. And he's really moving.

I shout, "Hey!" and he looks up, but he's not stopping, so I grab Alicia's arm and pull her to the right just in time to keep her from getting nailed. And as I pull her out of the way, she lets go of my elbow and puts her hand out to catch herself.

The kid shouts " 'Hey' yourself, lady!" and flips us the bird as he zooms off along the sidewalk.

So we make it to the other curb, and we're not dead, and nobody's too near, so I say, "Close call . . . sorry about that. Some kid on a scooter. You all right?"

And I look at her face, and she's not all right, not at all. There's a look on her face, a little scared, partly confused, partly something else. Like disgusted. And I know why. Because when I yanked her off balance and she put her hand out, her open hand went right up against my rib cage, almost into my left armpit. And she knows what bare skin feels like.

"You don't have a *shirt* on?" It's not a question. She

takes a half step back and says, "I mean, I thought it was weird when I took your elbow and you didn't have long sleeves or a jacket, but I just figured you were wearing a T-shirt or something because it was so warm earlier. But, like . . . like, even back in the *library*? How can you not have a *shirt* on in the library? And out here? It's cold now! It's *February*!"

And I can't deal with this. Not now. I can't stand here on the street corner and tell her that as weird as she thinks it is, it's actually ten times stranger than that, a hundred times stranger.

"What's going on? Talk to me. Are you there?"

I gulp. "Yeah. I'm here. But look, can I try to explain this later? Like, could I call you at home? It's not what you think."

Her face becomes fierce, a mask, almost primitive. "It's not what I think? So now you know what I think, is that it? Believe me, you *don't*. Because right now I think that for the last half hour I've been hanging out with some strange guy with no shirt on who's probably covered with tattoos, and I bet you have some piercings and some terrific body jewelry, right? So just get away from me, Bobby Phillips—if that's even your real name. You're not the first creep to try to pick up a cute little blind girl, and I'm not stupid. I know exactly where I am. This is *my* neighborhood, and I am walking home now. Alone. And if you come near me, like if I even *think* you're near me, I'll scream. And every shop owner and everybody who lives along this street knows who I am, and they'll be out here to bust you in a second. So go! Now! Go, and let me hear you yell good-bye from the other side of the avenue. Now!"

I don't say anything because a lady is walking past us, frightened of this blind girl who seems to be yelling at no one. If I were even a little bit guilty of anything, I'd just walk away. If I hadn't told her my name, and that my mom works for the university, if she had no way to trace me, I'd just walk away. Which would be the smart thing to do. Even now. But now I'm mad too, because she has no right to yell at me. I haven't done anything wrong, I haven't lied to her. And I'm not going to. I'm *not* a creep, and I won't let her think that about me for the rest of her life.

So I say, "Go ahead. Go ahead and scream. Scream all you want. I'll stand right over here. About ten feet away. And when you're done screaming and everyone comes to help you, and they come and try to haul me away, and they can't even *find* me—right on this corner—*then* maybe I'll tell you what's really going on. Because you don't have a clue, not a clue. No one does. So go ahead and scream. Let's see what happens."

That face of hers. It's running through about ten emotions a second. But there's one emotion taking charge. It's the fear. Like me on that first night at home. Alicia's alone in the dark, and she's afraid. And it just keeps building. She sucks in this huge breath, and I think she's really going to do it, just scream bloody murder. But she holds the breath for five seconds, ten seconds. Then she lets it hiss out slowly.

Her voice is hard and flat. "So tell me. Tell me the

truth. Tell me the big secret. Tell me how come you're not some shirtless creep." She's gripping her white cane with both hands, ready to use it like a samurai sword.

"Simple. Because I'm not just shirtless. I'm also pantsless and boxerless and sockless and shoeless. I'm not wearing any clothes at all. You wanted the truth, and I swear to God that's what I'm telling you. And if I'm telling you the truth—that I'm naked—then how come there's not a huge crowd standing around us right this minute? How come?"

She's really confused now, and even more afraid. So I say, "One possible reason a completely naked person is not drawing a crowd would be that everyone is as blind as you are. And the only other reason isn't even *possible:* That would be that no one can see me. So which do you think it is, Alicia? Is everyone around us blind, or am I . . . invisible?"

It's like I've just slapped her across the mouth. She comes to a full stop. Then furious, she hisses, "Very funny. Oh, look, look," she says, her voice dripping bitterness. She jerks her hand up and holds it in front of her face and acts like she's opening her eyes extra wide. "Well, well, well—I'm *invisible* too." Ice and granite and stainless steel. "Why don't you just take your sick humor and go away . . . Bobby." She practically spits the name into my face.

Alicia doesn't know what to do. And again, I think she might just start screaming. Instead, she takes her right hand off her cane and holds it out toward me. Her hand is trembling. "Here, let me hold your hand." Her voice is shaky now, but she sure has guts. I don't know what I'd be doing if our places were reversed—probably be screaming by now. I put my hand on her palm, and she clamps on to it. It's a powerful grip for such delicate-looking fingers. "Is anyone walking toward us?"

I scan the sidewalk. "Yeah. There's a guy just coming out of the Starbucks. He'll be here in about fifteen seconds."

"When he's right next to us, you squeeze my hand once, okay?"

I gulp, because she's really got a grip, and if she's going to try to get this guy to call a cop or something, then I'm going to have to work to get loose. But I say, "Fine. Whatever you say." Because I want her to know I'm not lying.

The guy is almost next to us, and I squeeze her hand.

"Excuse me, sir?" She's cute and she's good at asking for help, and the guy stops.

In a voice that's louder than it needs to be, the man says, "Yes? Can I help you, miss? Do you need to get across the street?"

My heart is jumping around in my chest, and I'm tensed, ready to cut and run. Alicia smiles at the man and says, "This guy here next to me, can you tell me if he's taller than I am? We've been having an argument because I think I'm taller than he is. What do you think?" Her hand tightens around mine.

The man is torn. He doesn't see a thing. I can tell this guy is worried that he's going to hurt this blind girl's feelings. But he clears his throat, and he says, "The guy there next to you? Miss . . . actually, there's no one there."

She shakes my hand like a puppy shaking a rag. "He's right here—I'm holding his hand! Who's taller, can't you tell?" Her voice is shrill, almost frantic.

The guy doesn't like being called a liar. "Miss, whoever you thought was there next to you, he's not there now. And I've got to go before the light changes." And he cuts across Fifty-seventh Street, glancing back once, shaking his head.

And now there's a new look on her face. New for Alicia. But I've seen it before. On Mom's and Dad's faces that first morning. It's the look of someone who's trying to process impossible information.

Because when something impossible happens, everything else comes unglued.

She's having trouble breathing. Then the first words. "So . . . you're, you're really—"

"Yeah," I say. "Invisible."

Then she finishes her sentence. "—*naked*?"

And I have to laugh a little, and I say, "Yeah, that too."

"And . . . and you're not some creep, like you're really Bobby Phillips and you go to the lab school and your mom teaches literature, just like you said? And this is really happening to you? Like, for real?"

"Really," I say. "I'm not making this up. How could I? You heard that guy. He couldn't see me. No one can if I don't wear clothes. And I came out without clothes today because, well, because the only other way is to get completely covered up—like I was on Tuesday. Except earlier today, it wasn't cold enough for that. And I had to get out of the house for a while. I had to."

Then I say, "Look, can we move over closer to the buildings? Because people keep coming past us, and you look funny here talking to no one. Over here."

She nods and follows my voice, tapping with her cane until she reaches the wall, looking sort of dazed. She's shaking her head. "But how . . . did it happen? Like, why you?"

I give an involuntary shrug. "That's what I've got to find out, and I have no idea." And again, that fact hits me like a bus. "I have no idea—and neither does my dad. He's a science wonk. He sounds a lot like your dad, maybe worse. He's real smart, and he doesn't even have a theory. Only me and my mom and my dad know about this. And now you."

She's standing there next to a drugstore window, the sharp breeze blowing her hair across her face, and she's trying to get her mind around it all. And she's doing a lot better than my parents did.

A sudden blast of frigid air hits us from the east, and she shivers. Then this look comes over her face. It's a mom look. And in a mom voice she says, "You must be freezing."

"Yeah, but everything's pretty intense for me right about now, so I don't think about it much."

"You want some cocoa? They have good cocoa at Starbucks. Really, you need to warm up. Here, put your left hand on my cane out there in front of mine, and you can just walk in with me. Everyone gets out of my way. Let's go."

And she turns toward the coffee shop, and I hold the cane, and in we go. She buys a tall cup of cocoa and asks for two straws. I steer her to a pair of stools against the wall. She pops the top off the cup and puts both straws into the drink. I start to bend toward the right-hand straw, but she whispers, "Too hot. It's always too hot. Just stir it for a minute or two."

There's a man at a small table about three feet from us. He glances up when he hears Alicia whisper, but immediately looks back to his newspaper. I guess blind people are allowed to whisper to themselves if they want to. Probably anybody is.

When the cocoa's drained down to the sweet dark stuff at the bottom of the cup, we get up and walk back outside, then to the corner. The clock on the bank across the street says it's 4:28, 58 degrees.

Alicia says, "Sorry I got so mad. I'm always getting mad."

I say, "Me too." Then I say, "I've got to get home. My mom's probably tried to call about ten times, and I've got to let her know I'm okay before she calls the National Guard or something. Except she can't, because we're not telling anyone about this. My dad thinks I'd get abducted by the government or something, and he's probably right. He'll go nuts if he finds out I told you. So you've got to keep this a secret, okay?"

She nods, dead serious. "Absolutely." Then a thought runs across her face and she grins. "But don't worry.

'Cause if I go to my mom or dad—or anybody—and I say, 'Hey, guess what! I drank some cocoa today with this invisible boy,' who do you think is going to have a problem—you or me?"

I laugh a little and then say, "Listen, I've got to go."

She says, "I'll be in that room again tomorrow from one to three. And if you want to call sometime, my last name is Van Dorn."

"Good. I'll try to come tomorrow. Maybe about two, okay?"

And she smiles and says, "Good."

"See y' Alicia."

"Bye, Bobby."

When I'm on the other side of Ellis, I look back. Alicia's walking away, working the long white cane, heading home.

I turn and start jogging, and I feel strong. I am the Greek warrior. And I know exactly what this soldier is going to do when he gets back to the barracks.

He's going to take a long, hot bath.

And as I trot along, I'm doing something I haven't felt like doing for at least two days.

I'm smiling.

chapter 12

A FRIEND

I come in the side door, and the phone's ringing.

"Bobby? What's going on? Are you all right? I've called six times during the past two hours, and your father's tried too. Where have you been?"

"Out."

"What does that mean? Out where?"

"Out. You know, out. Outside. Like not inside. It's a nice day, so I went out."

"But . . . but how?"

"Well, I walked down the steps to the side door, then I turned the doorknob, then I pulled on the door, and then I stepped over the threshold, and there I was. I was out."

Mom is quiet. Sarcasm makes Dad get loud. Mom gets quiet.

"So . . . where did you go?"

"All over."

"Did you walk?"

"On my very own feet. They work just fine."

"But how did you deal with—"

"With my little problem? Simple. The sun was shining earlier, and it didn't feel that cold, so I just stripped down to nothing and I went out."

Silence. "I wish you had told me. Or your dad. We need to know where you are, Bobby."

"You need to know where I am? Because you don't think I'm a responsible person? Well, I am. I know how to take care of myself. I'm actually pretty good at it."

Silence again. Plus a sniffle. "I should be home tomorrow, Bobby. Probably about noon. They've decided my nose won't need surgery, so that's good, I guess. Not that my nose has ever been some grand thing to be admired."

Mom wants to have a conversation, but I don't. "So you'll be home around noon?"

"Yes."

"Then I'll see you when you get here."

"Good."

"Okay. Well, I got kind of cold outside, and I just got back, and I need a bath now. So I'll see you tomorrow."

"All right, Bobby. Have a good night. And call if you need to talk to someone. Bobby . . . your dad and I love you very much. We do."

"Yup."

"Good-bye, Bobby."

"Bye."

As I hang up, I know I should have been nicer. I know she's just trying to be a good mom. But that's not what I need right now.

It's later, after a great bath, after some microwave lasagna and two root beers, after I've played my trumpet until my lips hurt, after I've watched the last half of *The Terminator* on cable: The phone rings.

It's right next to me on the couch, but I let it ring. Mom. Maybe Dad. I don't want to talk to either of them.

I grab the handset just before the answering machine kicks in.

"Yeah?"

A pause, about three seconds of silence. "'*Yeah?*' Is that how you answer the phone?" It's Alicia.

"Oh! Well, no. I mean, no one calls except my mom and dad. And I'm pretty tired of talking to them."

She says, "Then I'll try again."

And she hangs up.

Fifteen seconds later the phone rings. And I'm ready.

"Good evening, this is the Phillips residence, Bobby speaking."

She giggles. "Much better. Dignified, yet not too stuffy. Now, if you'd said 'Robert speaking,' that would have been too much." Then, in a quieter voice, "So, how are you? Did you thaw out?"

"Yeah. Completely. I love our hot water heater. It's one of the greatest inventions."

"Could be." There's a smile in her voice. "But I think the toilet ranks higher."

I'm nodding. "Right. Plumbing in general. Very good ideas. So, how are you?"

"Bored. My ears are worn out. You can only listen to so many audiobooks before everything starts to sound like mush."

Then I don't know what to say. I haven't had much practice talking to girls, not this week—not ever, really.

But I ask, "So, how bad did I scare you today?"

Because that's something I want to know. Like, how big a freak am I, really?

Alicia's quiet for a few seconds. "It's all I've been thinking about, I mean, about no one being able to see you. And I still don't know if I totally believe it's true—but it has to be. That guy didn't see you, and I know you were there. I waved your arm right in his face, and he didn't see a thing."

She asks me about when I bumped into her on Tuesday, like, what I was doing and how I got to the library, and I tell her about my first trip out, and about the two men in the fifth-floor bathroom, and then about the accident and me going to the hospital.

When I tell her about tube lady in the bed next to my mom's, she starts laughing and tells me I'm making it up. She laughs so hard that she makes those funny little snorts when she tries to breathe in.

Then she stops laughing. And she says, "I think you're so brave, Bobby. Really. Like, to go and visit your mom? And this afternoon, telling me about what's going on? That was brave too."

I can see the look on her face when she says that, and I can feel myself blushing. "Nah, you just got me mad, that's all. You were calling me a pervert, remember? And I didn't want you to think that."

Another dead end, both of us feeling awkward. Or maybe it's just me, blushing my patented invisible blush.

She breaks the vacuum with a question. "So, will you come to the library tomorrow?"

"I said I'd try, remember?"

"Yeah, but how hard are you going to try?"

"Have to see. My mom's coming home from the hospital about twelve. So I don't know what's gonna be happening here around two. Could be all hell breaking loose. But I'll try to come, I really will."

"So it's a definite maybe."

"Yup."

"Okay. Bye, Bobby."

"Bye. . . . Oh—Alicia?"

"Yes?"

"Thanks for calling."

"You're welcome."

"Bye."

I'm sitting on the couch next to an empty lasagna tin and two root beer bottles, but I'm a million miles away. Or maybe only about ten blocks away. I can see what Alicia's face looks like, and I can see her smile, and then the phone rings.

Another courtesy test.

I grab it on the first ring and say, "Good evening, Miss Van Dorn. You've reached the Phillips residence again."

"Bobby?"

"Dad! Hey . . . hi, Dad. How's it going?" I try to sound cheerful, but I didn't want it to be Dad. Because talking to Dad snaps my missing body back into focus, and for a few minutes I'd forgotten all that.

" 'Miss Van Dorn,' " Dad says, "who's Miss Van Dorn?"

"Someone you don't know, Dad. A friend of mine." I talk to Dad for about five minutes, but I'm not thinking about what's he's saying.

I'm thinking about what I just said about Alicia. About how she's a friend. And about how it's true.

Because, already, that's what Alicia is. She's a friend.

chapter 13

TRUSTING

I t's Friday about 12:45 when Mom gets home from the hospital. I'd like to go help her out of the cab, but I can't, so the driver holds her arm and helps her up the front steps. I don't like seeing her move so stiffly, like an old person. I open the door for her, and when it's shut, we hug. And I'm actually glad to see her.

Then Mom walks slowly around the first floor. I can tell she's not happy with the way the kitchen looks. Or the TV room. Or anything. That's because she had to call from the hospital and cancel our cleaning service, and she had to do that because of me. But Mom is good. I can tell she wants to start giving orders, but she doesn't, and I'm impressed. All she says is, "Maybe you could help me get things straightened up a little."

So I do. I get out the vacuum cleaner and go to work.

But about 1:30, I tell her I'm going out. We're standing in the kitchen, and she's got a sponge mop in her hands, slowly working on a little spilled ice cream. She looks in my direction.

"What do you mean?" And her tone of voice is like the old Mom, the Director. So I shoot off some sarcasm—old Mom, old Bobby.

"Remember what I told you yesterday, Mom? Out means out. Outside. Out of the house. Somewhere that is not here. I'm going out."

"But why?"

Before I think, I say, "Because I'm going to meet someone at the library." The look on Mom's face shows me how stupid I am.

"Who? You haven't told anyone about what's happening, have you?"

I'm a rotten liar, even when people can't see my face. And besides, why should I have to lie? So I take a deep breath and say, "Yes, I have. I met a girl, a blind girl. And she knows about everything, but it's okay. She's not going to tell anyone, and like she said to me, no one would believe her if she did."

Mom grabs the back of a chair with both hands, and the mop handle clatters to the floor. She starts shaking her head. "Robert, Robert, Robert . . . you promised your father you wouldn't tell a soul, right here in this room. He's going to be so upset about this. And, and I'm *very* disappointed in you. Why in the world did you tell her?"

"Why? Because *I* decided I needed to tell her. It was a special situation, and *I* decided *I* could trust her."

"Have you known this girl long?"

"Since Tuesday."

Mom almost shouts, "Since Tuesday? *This* Tuesday? Oh, Robert. This . . . this is like trusting a total stranger with your life!"

"Exactly! And that's the part you and Dad still don't get: It's *my* life! And if I want to talk to someone and trust someone, then I'm going to, no matter what you think. It's *my* decision, not yours!"

So that's the mood I leave the house in. And I'm stupid again, because I just yank off my clothes in the back stairwell and run outside. Stupid, because even though it's the warmest part of the day and it's sunny, the temperature's only about 42 degrees. It's a case of run or die, so I cover the half mile to the library in record time. And by the time I get my breathing under control and go up to the third floor, it's almost two.

Then I'm there, and I'm looking in through the glass in the door to the listening room, and I'm glad I came. She's sitting there, right where she was yesterday, her long fingers hovering above the keys of her laptop, head tilted to one side, listening. She's got on a dark green sweater and some reddish corduroy pants. There's a thin strand of pearls around her neck. She looks dressed up, prettier than ever. Somebody knows what looks good on this girl.

Then I gulp. Because she looks like she's dressed . . . for a date.

I tap and open the door, step inside, shut it behind me.

"Hi."

"Bobby—hi." She smiles. A careful smile. She shuts off the tape player. It's still Hawthorne. "So, did your mom get home?"

"Yeah." I feel like I shouldn't be here. And I feel naked. Alone with a blind girl and very naked. Nothing in life prepares a guy for that, not even pretending to be a Greek warrior. I don't sit down. I just stand across the wide oak table from her, my hands on the back of a chair.

Alicia's on edge too. She isn't going to let the conversation slow down. She says, "So, how is she? And what about your dad?"

"My dad wanted to come home too, but the doctors wouldn't let him. Which is good. See, what I hope is that he has to stay away long enough that when he gets out, he can go right back to work. I don't think I could stand being stuck in the house all day with both my folks."

Alicia is nodding as if what I'm saying is really interesting to her. But I've stopped talking, so she gives me another prompt. "And your mom, she's at home now, right?"

I'm glad for the help, because all of a sudden silence seems scary. I mean, what Mom said was kind of true. I hardly know this girl. And when I talk, I feel like my voice sounds funny. "Yeah, she's home. She's okay, but she's still kind of weak. The taxi guy had to help her up the front steps when she got home. And then the second she got in the house, I had to do some cleaning 'cause I could tell she was grossed out. I mean, I didn't do any dusting or anything while she was gone, but still, it was only three days. It's not like the house was a pit or something."

While I'm talking, I glance at the door of the listening room. There's a guy there at the window, a man in a tweed jacket, about forty years old with a big head of wild hair. He stops, looks in, sees Alicia, looks at his watch, and then walks on.

Alicia nods. "Yeah, my mom's the same way. And my dad too. Neatness freaks. And now that I can't see anything, it's even worse. They're afraid for me all the time, like if a shoe is lying in the wrong place, they think I'm going to trip over it and break my neck."

I pounce on that idea. "You said you've been blind for two years, right?" Because that's something we haven't talked about yet.

She nods. "Uh-huh. A little more than two years now."

"I asked about that yesterday, but you didn't tell me how it happened."

She shrugs and blushes a little. "It just happened, that's the dumb part. It's not like there was some disease, or a terrible accident or anything."

"But, like, something had to happen, right?"

Her upper lip curls into a little sneer. She snaps, "Yeah, well, duh, Bobby—I mean, *something* happened. Of course something happened."

I don't know what to say. Talking with her, it's like walking along on ice, and I think it's safe, and then I take one more step, and everything starts to crack and buckle. And under the ice there's this dark river.

We're both quiet. Then she takes a deep breath and lets it out slowly. And she smiles a little. "Sorry. It's just I don't know how to tell about it. I think about this stuff, but I don't talk about it."

I look at her face the whole time, and I can see her thinking, deciding if she wants to talk. And it's like she's going a long way back somewhere so she can look around and remember. Then in a quiet little voice I have not heard before, she starts talking.

"It just happened. Two years ago. It was night, it was cold, January nineteenth, two days before my birthday. My mom had left the window open. I remember being really cold and waking up without any covers on. I reached over the side of the bed where they usually fall off, and they weren't there, so I reached toward the other side, toward the windows. And I fell out of bed. I just fell and hit my head. I didn't think anything about it. It didn't even hurt that much. I just got up and kind of shook it off."

She pauses. This is hard for her. But she keeps going, talking in that small voice. "I wasn't really awake, so I just grabbed my quilts off the floor and pulled them around me and went back to sleep. But in the morning . . . the morning was horrible. I knew I was awake, but it was like I was still asleep, or like I was lost inside this big dark . . . thing. But I knew I was home, in my own room. I could hear the birds on the feeder outside, and I could feel the sun on my face at the window, feel the cold glass on my fingertips, but . . . I couldn't see anything."

The guy in the tweed jacket is back at the door of the room. Must be waiting for a seminar meeting. He looks in, acts as if he's going to open the door, then leaves again.

Alicia takes a long ragged breath, and then wills herself to calm down. "You remember how mad I got yesterday when you said you were invisible?"

"Yeah."

"Well, part of that was because that's exactly how I

105

felt that first morning, that whole first year when I was suddenly the little blind girl. It was like I became invisible. I couldn't see myself, I couldn't see me going to dances or college or grad school, couldn't see myself becoming an archaeologist. I was never going to get to see the pyramids or the Valley of the Kings. And I couldn't even see getting married or having kids, or anything I used to wish about. Everything just disappeared.

"I could tell other people were looking at me funny, I could feel it, and I could hear it in their voices. It felt like they wished I would just go away. I made them uncomfortable. And I couldn't read the books I loved, I couldn't watch movies, couldn't see sunsets or flowers. It was all invisible, just like me.

"Like a million different doctors looked at my eyes, and they were all real nice, and they explained what happened, but everyone said it couldn't be fixed.

"And it was like my parents couldn't see me either. They just saw this thing that was suddenly helpless. They're better now, but still, I'm not their wonderful daughter they were so proud of anymore. Now I'm a big job, a job they can't get rid of even if they wanted to." Anger again. Deep and hot and hurtful.

Out of the corner of my eye, I notice the man again, the guy with the big hair. He's about four feet back from the door, and he looks anxious. He's got an old tan briefcase in one hand. He's standing at an angle where he can see Alicia as she talks. Then he moves, trying to scan the room to see the person who's listening to her. I think, *Get lost, mister. The room's reserved until three, and if this girl wants to talk to the walls, that's what she's gonna do.*

"What about your friends?" I ask. "Didn't they help?"

Her lower lip trembles, and maybe this is one question too many. I really can't take tears. But she pulls back from the edge, and she starts talking again.

"I guess I was popular before it happened, but that didn't help. All the kids I hung around with just disappeared—all but Nancy, Nancy Fredericks. She was great. She came over almost every day after school, and she talked, and she just sat there and took it if I got mad and started calling her terrible names, and when I cried sometimes, she cried too. She could still see me, and she didn't care about the blindness. That first year, my parents had special tutors come to our house and start to teach me Braille and all that blind junk—you know, like, 'Here's your white cane to tap around with, little girl.' But it was Nancy who kept me from going crazy. She told me about school and the teachers and the boys, and who had a crush on who. We still talk on the phone. It's like she's the only thing that didn't change in my life. Everything and everybody else changed. . . . It's like I disappeared along with the whole rest of the world."

She's done. And she's self-conscious again. I don't know what to say. I feel like I've been reading her diary. Risky stuff. So I just say, "Thanks . . . for telling me all that."

"Why thanks?" she asks. She sits back in her chair and pulls her legs up against her chest.

"I don't know," I say, "I guess, because you didn't have to tell me."

She gets a devilish smile on her face. "Like yesterday, when you didn't *have* to tell me about what's happening to you, right?"

"Yeah. Like that."

And then I see what she means. Because I *did* have to tell her, just like she had to tell me all of this. I had to trust her. Sometimes you have to tell someone else what it's like. Because if you don't, you'll go nuts.

The tweedy guy is at the door again, and now he's pushing it open, barging right in. Alicia hears the door and turns, putting her feet down as she does.

The man says, "Alicia? What are you doing? Who are you talking to?"

The color drains from Alicia's face. She says, "Wh . . . what are you doing here?"

"I'm here because your mom called and said she thought you might be meeting someone here today, and—"

"And you thought it would be all right to do a little spying on your little girl, is that it?" Alicia presses her lips together. She's past the surprise already, and now she's mad.

And me? I'm scared. Because I'm shut inside a small room with a blind girl and her father.

And the man is looking for answers.

chapter 14

TWO COMMITTEES

So Alicia's dad finds out about me, and then her mom does too. It's not much of a story. It's Friday in the library, and Alicia's taking heat from her dad about why she's talking to the wall for five minutes straight, and I can see that she's going to have to start lying for me. And I don't want her to have to do that. So I just begin talking to her dad.

And he stutters, and squints, and passes through all the phases that Mom, Dad, and Alicia have: fear, confusion, disbelief, and then amazement that levels out to a steady curiosity. Of course, for Mom and Dad, the final phase is a steady worry that keeps on chewing at them—but that's because they're my parents, and parents can't help worrying about their kids, even if they're fine.

So as the great Professor Leo Van Dorn gets over the shock, he immediately starts to theorize, just like my dad did, except that he's an astronomer, so instead of talking calmly about visible light anomalies and refractive indexes like Dad did, he's pacing around the room looking at me from every angle while he runs one hand through his Einstein hair, and he's saying that I'm like a black hole, ". . . a different absorptive principle, of course, but quite extraordinary nevertheless."

The next person who has to know is Alicia's mom. After all, you can't have two thirds of a family knowing a juicy secret like The Bobby Story. So as they leave the library, I tell Alicia and her dad it's okay to tell Mrs. Van Dorn, as long as they're sure she won't go nuts and call the cops or something. And late Friday afternoon Alicia's mom passes through the same steps when Alicia and her dad tell her about me. I hear about it later on the phone from Alicia. First her mom thinks Alicia and her dad are ganging up on her to play a practical joke. When she finally believes them, she goes right to the heart of her problem with the whole situation. She says to Alicia, "What does this young man *wear* when you meet with him?"

And Alicia says, "On really cold days, he wears Saran Wrap, but most of the time he's naked." Mrs. Van Dorn is not amused by this.

And my first visit to Alicia's house? That's on Saturday afternoon. It didn't help that Alicia didn't tell her mom that I was coming. I ring the doorbell, and I think it's going to be Alicia, and it's this lady in an exercise leotard with her hair up in a headband. Alicia's standing behind her, grinning toward the doorway. And her mom looks around, up and down the sidewalk, and she gets this angry flash in her eyes, and she's about to slam the door shut when I say, "Mrs. Van Dorn? I'm Bobby Phillips. Alicia said I could come over to see her today." And her mom's eyes bug out, and she steps back and gasps, and she doesn't know what to do. Which is when Alicia pipes up and says, "Sorry, Mom, I forgot to tell you. It's okay, isn't it? If Bobby comes in for a while?" And I can tell by the look on Alicia's face that she did it on purpose, surprising her mom and me. Her mom lets me in, but she says, "Stand right there," and she runs—really runs—and brings me a long white terry cloth robe to wear.

And that first visit, Alicia sits on a chair in the living room, and I sit on the couch with her mom, and she stays there with us the whole time.

And I don't blame her. If Alicia were my daughter, I'd want to protect her too.

Mom is wrong about Dad being so mad that I'm telling other people about the "situation." She said I had to tell him about the Van Dorns myself. When I call him at the hospital late Saturday afternoon, I'm all set for a big yelling match. It doesn't happen. Dad listens when I tell him about Alicia, and about her dad and mom, and he doesn't shout or splutter or interrupt me or anything. He's quiet, and then he says, "If that's the decision you've made, Bobby, then your mom and I will back you up a hundred percent. These people might even end up being a help. Frankly, I've been feeling a little over-whelmed about everything. I've heard of Professor Van Dorn, and I can't wait to meet him and talk about this." I'm surprised he takes the news so well, and as I hang up, I wonder why he's so mellow, and I wonder if this is a real change. But I don't get my hopes up too high. It might just be something the doctor is piping into his brain.

I know what Dad means about feeling overwhelmed,

and he's right—it's a relief to have a few more people on the official Save Bobby Phillips Committee. Because this started on Tuesday, and now it's Saturday—that's five days.

When I woke up this morning, I got scared. Not scared like the last four mornings. Not scared by the sudden rediscovery that my body is missing. I got scared because I woke up already knowing that I'm like this. That means I'm getting used to it. Nothing's changing, and I'm just rolling along, going with the flow. I'm adjusting to a serious maladjustment!

And that's truly frightening. But I'm learning stuff.

The real lessons start two weeks later when Dad comes home from the hospital. And he's at home with me and Mom for six days before he starts commuting to Batavia again. He's got a blue plastic cast on his left arm from his elbow to his knuckles. Most of the time at home he spends poking through a huge stack of books and scientific journals. And now that he's going to FermiLab every day, I have the feeling he's doing the same thing there all day. Looking for the science of what's happening. I reminded him about maybe taking a fingernail clipping to put under the electron microscope, but he shook his head and said, "Too early for that. Need to have a better theoretical grip on it first."

And Dad's different. Or maybe I am. Or maybe it's both of us, because there's a lot less yelling. He talks, I listen. I talk, he listens. He still says plenty of stupid stuff, and he still says "bingo" way too much. But he's definitely not the same person.

So one thing I learn is that maybe everyone should have a near-death experience now and then. Sure did the trick for Dad.

And I learn that I can have a girlfriend. Or at least a friend who's a girl. That's because I talk to Alicia a lot. We talk on the phone, and we do instant messaging. She's got a text-to-speech translator on her PC, so whatever I type into a message window, her PC says out loud. She types a lot faster than I do. And we just talk.

She tells me how her day stinks, or how her mom yells at her, and I tell her how my day stinks and how my mom yells at me. She tells me that the week before she went blind, she checked a book out of the library called *Welcome to the Monkey House*. It's by Kurt Vonnegut, and she only read the first three stories, and now her audiobook supplier can't find a recording of it. So we talk about Vonnegut and I tell her that my favorite book of his is *Cat's Cradle*. Then I get my mom to buy the *Monkey House* book, and I read Alicia a couple of the stories over the phone. She says I'm really good at reading aloud. And we just talk about stuff. So that's something I learn I can do.

Because, before Alicia, what girls did I actually talk to? There's Mom. And then there's about fifty teachers and baby-sitters and day-care ladies who are all basically like Mom. There's Carla, who was my lab partner in eighth-grade science, and she's basically like Dad. And that's pretty much it. So my known-female database is pretty limited. Because the girls at the lab school are mostly scary. And if any of them want to be friends, they haven't told me. About half of the girls at U High act like they've known what they want to do in life since about third grade. Girls like Meaghan Murray and Lida Strauss? If they see me at all, they look at me like I'm a bug, something to squash as they march toward the highest possible class rank. The other half of the girls have money. Girls like Jessica and her crew. They're into clothes and shoes and jewelry and cell phones and beepers—and cars will be next. These girls don't pass notes in class. They send infrared e-mails to each other on little palm computers.

There is Kendra, though. I've talked with her. She plays tenor sax in the jazz band. This solo she plays on "Harlem Nocturne"? It's so good, it makes me want to take sax lessons. I talk with her once in a while, just talk. Still, Kendra's more like a musician than a girl.

So like I said, because of Alicia, I learn that a girl will talk to me, and even seem to enjoy it. We both enjoy it.

Back at the end of the first week when I told Dr. Van Dorn and he got so excited, I thought he and Dad—and the Committee—would get together right away. Do some big-league brainstorming. Work up an action plan to Save Bobby Phillips. It doesn't happen. But the Committee does agree on one thing—by phone—that if Bobby Phillips is ever going to have a regular life, we must maintain absolute secrecy while we look for a way to get him back to normal.

So I learn the hard way that I shouldn't depend on a committee to solve my problems.

Sitting on my bed looking at my bookcase one night

during the second week, I see my thick Sherlock Holmes collection. It's all the stories in two fat volumes. The great thing about Sherlock Holmes is, he never sat around looking for theories. He was into the facts. And observation. Like in "The Adventure of the Speckled Band"? About the man who dies in his bed one night, and no one can figure it out? It's because no one took the time to really look at the room. And when Holmes does, he sees exactly what happened.

That idea sets me off, and over the next few days, whenever I'm not talking to my folks or Alicia or not eating or sleeping, I'm being a detective. I start by writing down everything I can remember about the two days before the suspect disappeared. What the suspect ate, what he wore, where he went, who he talked to, where he sat, how many times he washed his hands—as much as I can remember. And I tape four sheets of typing paper together end to end and lay all the information out on a time line, hour by hour. Because there must be a clue somewhere. People don't just disappear. Something—or someone—had to make it happen.

Then I start to think of my room like it's a crime scene. Because that's where I was when it happened. Or maybe I was in the hall bathroom. So I make a list of everything in both rooms. Everything. The carpet and the lightbulbs and my alarm clock and the flashlight under my bed and the pack of firecrackers hidden in my desk, the shampoo in the tub, the plunger under the sink, Dad's old Norelco razor, everything. Then I categorize every item as many different ways as I can think of. Natural, synthetic, liquid, solid, electrical, chemical, wood, metal, plastic, paper—on and on. And it feels like I'm making progress for a day or two. But by the end of the second week, I'm out of ideas, and no matter how I look at all the information, all I see is an invisible kid looking at nothing in a mirror. And when I show the lists and the time line to Dad after dinner one night, he says, "Hmmm. Interesting material, Bobby. I'll hang on to it." But I can tell from his face that Dad doesn't think much of my sleuthing.

So another thing I learn is that Sherlock Holmes always finds the right clue, and I don't.

Here's something dangerous I learn. About myself. I learn that even with a steady fear eating away at me—the fear of being this way forever—and even when I'm working hard to find a solution or just a clue, even then, I can call Alicia or get a snack or read a book, and I can trick myself into feeling almost normal for hours at a time.

But the most dangerous thing I learn during this three weeks is that people who run schools are nosy. They don't like it when a kid just stops coming. It doesn't matter if it's a public school or one like mine. When you don't show up for a week, they want to know the details.

So the school nurse calls the Monday after my mom gets home from the hospital. Mom tells her I've still got the flu. The nurse has heard about the car accident, that Mom and Dad were in the hospital. Mom tells her that Aunt Ethel was here to take care of me. The nurse is glad I'm doing much better now—how much longer will he be missing classes? Another week? Fine.

A week later—to the day—the nurse is not curious anymore. Now she's edgy. She calls Mom again. She's getting notes from my teachers and the counseling office, because two weeks is a long time to be absent from a high-powered private prep school. It's a lot of classes to miss, not to mention the midterm exams. And Mom chats and tells her not to worry, that Bobby is much better now.

Then a half hour later on the same day, Mr. Creed, the guidance counselor, calls Mom and says he's got a huge pile of books and assignments for me. He'd be happy to bring them over to the house. And if the flu isn't infectious anymore, maybe he could talk with Bobby and explain some of the assignments. But Mom says no, don't bother, she'll be happy to stop in at the office, because Bobby is still tired a lot. And the counselor says it would be good if the school could have a note from our family doctor about the illness. Just for the files. Because that's the school policy about long absences. When there's a note in the file, the work can be made up gradually with no penalties.

But Mom and Dad don't have a note from Dr. Weston. Because that would mean a house call. Dr. Weston's bedside manner is a little too gossipy, a little too informal for Dad. Dad doesn't want Dr. Weston anywhere near me.

So there's no note.

The next day, Mom calls Mr. Creed and then goes to pick up my assignments. Her black eyes have turned to a bruised yellow, so no one stares too much when she goes to the counseling center. But when Mom is talking with Mr. Creed, and the school nurse happens to pass by—"Mrs. Phillips, isn't it? And how's that Bobby? He has the flu, right?"—it doesn't feel like a coincidence.

Schools aren't in the business of wondering about kids or guessing about kids. Schools are in the business of knowing, and when a school wants to find something out, the school takes steps. Private schools aren't linked up with the state government like the public schools are. They actually try to stay free of the state. But one of the ways private schools do that is by following all the rules. And the state has rules about children and extended illnesses and contagious diseases, and it doesn't matter what kind of a school the kid attends.

So that's why a second Save Bobby Phillips Committee gets going. At the beginning it's the nurse, my teachers, the guidance counselor, and the people who run the school.

Maybe it's the nurse or the counselor, or somebody else at school. Maybe it's nobody at the school. But it's somebody, and I vote for the nurse. Because *somebody* calls the Cook County Board of Health and reports that a fifteen-year-old boy attending University High School has been home *ill for three weeks.* The parents have not supplied a note from a doctor. No one has even seen the child—me, that is—during the past three weeks.

And then somebody at the Board of Health calls the Department of Children and Family Services. So the second Save Bobby Phillips Committee is getting bigger.

And *this* committee has an action plan.

chapter 15
A SMALL WAR

It's another Monday morning, and after three full weeks at home, a ringing doorbell is a major event in my life. So I drop *The Lord of the Rings* on my bed and trot to the landing at the top of the front hall staircase. I bend down to look, and I can see that Mom is standing in the front doorway. And I listen.

"Mrs. Phillips?"

"Yes?"

"How do you do. My name is Officer Martha Pagett, and I'm from the school and truancy division of the State Department of Children and Family Services. May I come in?"

"Is there a problem?" When Mom says that, I tiptoe to my room, pull off my clothes, and hustle down the back stairs. I want to see the action.

By the time I get up to the front of the house, Mom is still standing squarely in the doorway. She's not even going to let the woman into the front hall. I'm about four feet away, looking at them through the French doors that open to the front hall from the parlor.

The woman is shorter than Mom—most women are. She's got a narrow face, and her brown hair is pulled back into some kind of twisty thing. Thick lenses in her wire-frame glasses make her eyes look big. She's wearing a blue skirt and jacket. Her coat has a small American flag on the left lapel. Her white shirt is buttoned all the way up, and there's a black briefcase in her left hand.

The lady is smiling, nodding, talking, and Mom is listening, trying to look pleasant, her arms folded across her chest. ". . . so naturally, there's some concern about Bobby. I'm sure you'll agree that three weeks is an uncommonly long illness. Since the school has not received a note from a physician, we've been asked to make a visit and simply verify that Bobby's on the mend and that everything's fine at home."

So this isn't just a chat. This lady wants to see a body. My body.

I can see the wheels spinning behind Mom's eyes. She's smiling, and it looks like a real smile, but I know better. That's her I'm-just-barely-not-ripping-your-head-off smile.

Raising her eyebrows, still smiling, Mom says, "And you believe you have the authority to march up my front steps and into my home and ask to see my sick child? Is that what you're saying? Do you have a search warrant?"

This social worker doesn't know Emily Colton Phillips. For example, she doesn't know that Mom got pushed around by Chicago cops when she was eighteen during the 1968 Democratic Convention. And Mom pushed back. I've seen the news footage. Then two years later, she chained herself to the door of the university president's office. And she stayed there six days—until he promised to hire more women as professors.

The lady looks up at Mom. I can see her stiffen and

tighten her grip on the handle of her briefcase. She keeps smiling too, but I can see it's just a mask. I'm looking at a small war between two smart women. Without raising her voice, she says, "You mean today? Do I have a search warrant right now? No, Mrs. Phillips, not today. But I can assure you that I do have every right under the child protection laws of the state of Illinois to have a brief visit with your son, and if I need to have a search warrant to accomplish that, then I can certainly get one."

Mom waves her hand as if to whisk away that idea. "Oh, don't mind me, Miss Badger."

"It's Ms. Pagett," says the woman in blue.

Mom laughs lightly, still smiling. "Yes, Ms. Pagett. Please forgive me. I must sound like I'm ready to call a press conference and accuse you of being a jackbooted government thug or something. That's just my old radical upbringing talking. Of course you can talk to Bobby. You could talk to him right now, except for one problem—he's not here."

The lady looks surprised, almost as surprised as I am. She says, "Oh. I see. Do you mind my asking where he is?" She's stooping now, putting her briefcase flat on the porch floor. She opens it and takes out a pen and a yellow legal pad.

"Not at all. It's so cold and damp this time of year in Chicago. What with his illness and the accident and all, Mr. Phillips and I decided that some time away would be good for Bobby. He left Thursday to stay with a relative in Florida for a month or so."

Ms. Pagett is surprised again. "Florida?" She's standing up now, writing.

Mom nods, smiles sweetly. "Yes. We're withdrawing Bobby from school for the rest of this semester. He just missed his midterm exams, you know, and we don't want him to feel burdened with all that makeup work. It's just too much right now, and his health has to come first."

Scribbling on the yellow pad, the woman nods. "Yes, of course. And where in Florida will he be?"

Mom says, "Down in the southern part, where it's nice and warm."

The woman frowns slightly, but keeps writing, and without looking up she says, "And when do you expect Bobby to come home?"

With a shrug and a smile, Mom says, "Hard to say. Certainly not until he's feeling like his old self again. Now, Miss Pagett, is there anything else I can help you with this morning?"

The lady looks up into Mom's face, her eyes slightly narrowed, her lips pressed together. There's a pause, and the silence is filled with questions, questions like, "Where is he—really?" and "Do you know how fast I could have a search warrant?" and "You know this isn't over, don't you?"

Then she bends down to put her pad and pen back into the briefcase. The latches click, she straightens up, looks Mom in the face, and says, "I think that's all the help I need today, Mrs. Phillips. Thanks so much for your time."

Mom meets the lady's eyes, and smiles. They both know that round one is over. Mom won. "You're quite welcome. Bye now."

When the lady's heels have tapped across the wooden porch and down the steps, Mom turns around and calls softly, "Bobby?"

I open one of the French doors. "In here, Mom. So now I'm in Florida, huh? Cool."

"I can hear you smiling, Bobby, and you shouldn't be. This isn't funny." Mom moves quickly to the lace curtains on the front bay window and peeks out. "These people are like pit bulls. See that?"

I look over her shoulder, and the social worker is standing on the porch next door, talking with Mrs. Trent, taking notes.

"That lady is on a case. You are the case, Bobby. And your father and I. The school nurse and the Board of Health and the Department of Children and Family Services have got their little collective brain into a tizzy about one missing boy, and they're going to push until they get answers. This isn't funny."

But I think it is. "Right, so what do they think? Do they think you murdered me and put me down the garbage disposer or something? Or maybe I'm locked in a closet? Come on, Mom. Get real."

Mom isn't smiling. Her face is so pale that the bruises under her eyes look bright as goldfinches. Her lips are tight, her words clipped. "No, Robert, you get real. You do not understand this situation. This is not a joke. This is the state. These people have real power, and they are not afraid to use it. Kids do get hurt by their parents and others, and someone's got to be allowed to look around if things are suspicious. And right now, our situation looks very suspicious. It's not going to surprise me one bit if that woman and six of Chicago's finest come back here in one hour with a search warrant and complete authority to tear this house apart—looking for one Bobby Phillips, male Caucasian, age fifteen years, last seen by Mrs. Trent getting out of a cab on the evening his parents were involved in a car crash, when he was already supposedly home from school with a severe case of the flu. So don't laugh about this. This is a real mess— and it's dangerous for you. I don't want these people taking you away from me. And now I've got to call Aunt Ethel."

Mom runs to the den and calls her aunt and tells her that if she gets a contact from anyone asking about me, she's to say that I've been there since March thirteenth, and that I arrived by train. Or maybe it would be a good idea to let her answering machine screen the calls for the next week or so, because if you don't talk to anyone, you can't very well be charged with perjury. And, really, maybe the best idea is to go check into a nice hotel under her maiden name for a week or so—at our expense, of course—would she mind terribly? And if you want to talk, please call our cell phone number.

And when Aunt Ethel asks for details, Mom feels like she has to give them to her. So she takes about three minutes and tells the condensed version of how Bobby became a fugitive from the law.

And Aunt Ethel is the only one so far who isn't fazed by the idea of an invisible teenager. She says something like, "Well, isn't that curious! He must fly down here at once so he can be my bridge partner!" So now Great-Aunt Ethel is in on the secret.

Mom's wrong about one thing, though. It's when she says that the social worker could be back in an hour with a search warrant to tear the house apart.

Actually, it only takes Ms. Pagett forty-five minutes.

chapter 16

SEARCHING FOR
BOBBY PHILLIPS

I think Mom is nuts.

When the lady from Children and Family Services stops talking to Mrs. Trent, she gets in her car and drives away. Then Mom has this frantic phone conversation with Aunt Ethel, and the second she hangs up, she starts barking orders at me: "Robert, clean up your room. Put all your clothes away. Put all your books back on the shelves. Pack up your trumpet and put it on your closet shelf. Get your toothbrush out of the bathroom and put it . . . put it with the cleaning supplies under the sink. And toss your towel from this morning down the back stairs. Make your bed and be sure your electric blanket is turned off. Make your room look like no one has been there for days. Now, move it!"

And then she runs into the kitchen and starts washing the breakfast and lunch dishes like a maniac, doing them by hand and stacking them away instead of putting them into the dishwasher.

I'm halfway done with my room when Mom yells up the back stairs at me, "Bobby? Think carefully—did you send any e-mails or AOL messages since Wednesday?"

I think, then holler back, "Nope. I talked to Alicia on the phone a couple of times, but that's it."

"Good. As soon as you're done, I want you to run

126

down to the laundry room and get all the rest of your clothes. Fold the dirty ones neatly and put them away in your drawers too. Hurry!"

"Hey, Mom, really, lighten up a little."

"Bobby, I don't want any discussion. If I'm wrong about this, then that'll be wonderful. But for now, keep working!"

I think Mom is crazy—until forty minutes later when the lady comes back. Her blue sedan stops at the curb, and then two Chicago cop cars pull up behind her. Three officers get out, two men and a woman.

Ms. Pagett is at the door with the officers, and after Mom reads the search warrant, she walks into the den and calls Dad and then our lawyer, Charles Clarke. Mr. Clarke arrives in five minutes, but he doesn't do anything except read the warrant and tell Mom that everything's in order.

"What's this all about, Emily?"

Ms. Pagett is standing right there, so Mom says, "Nothing, Charlie. It's about nothing, and I'll call you later, okay? Thanks a lot for coming so quickly." And the lawyer shakes his head, smiles, and leaves.

Ms. Pagett is enjoying herself. This is round two, and Mom is getting beat up good. The three police officers fan out. Two go up, and one stays down with the social worker.

I follow the man and woman who go upstairs. They open the doors to all the rooms, figure out right away which one is mine, and then go in.

And I'm glad Mom is so smart. She called this one

right. My room looks empty, cleared out. They open the closet, they open every drawer. They look under the bed.

I'm out in the hall, watching. They're being careful, not trashing the place, not making a mess. Which is good. My room's neater than it's been in about three years, and I don't want to have to clean it up again.

They go to the hall bathroom. No toothbrush, no wet towels. There's a comb by the sink, but they don't focus on it.

They check every room, every closet, every cabinet. They open every drawer. They shine their long black flashlights into every space big enough to hide a kid about my size. They trudge up the attic stairs, poke around, and then track dark dust onto the hall carpet when they come down again.

When they're done, I follow them down the back stairs to the kitchen, but I don't go on down to the basement with them. In the den, Mom is sitting at the desk, doing her best to ignore the suit woman. But the lady is pushing.

"Mrs. Phillips, I must insist that you tell me where in Florida you have sent your son. Failure to freely offer information will not be viewed favorably."

Mom isn't even trying to smile now. "The terms of your search warrant are quite clear. You have permission to make a superficial survey of the premises in order to see if my son is here, which, as I had already told you, he is not. It is you, in collusion with some other misguided souls, who have chosen to make this a formal matter, and create this legal situation. As far as I am concerned, however, this is still a family matter over which you and the state of Illinois have no jurisdiction whatsoever. I am not under any obligation to tell you one thing more. I already told you that he has gone to Florida to stay with a relative while he recovers from a recent illness. We are withdrawing him from school, which we have every right to do. And I have nothing more to say."

"Maybe you can comment on this. Your neighbor, Mrs. Trent, tells us that while you and your husband were in the hospital, a person referred to as Aunt Ethel was here taking care of Bobby. Is this true?"

Mom's annoyed about Mrs. Trent getting involved, but she says, "Yes. That is correct."

"And is this the same aunt Ethel whose telephone number is on the list on the wall by your kitchen telephone?"

After a pause Mom says, "Yes." She's mad at herself for not taking that list off the wall.

I can see where Ms. Pagett is going, and so can Mom.

"Since I notice that this aunt Ethel is the only person on your list with a south Florida area code, I know you won't mind if we give her a call, just to see if Bobby is there. And if he does happen to be there, then my agency will exercise our reciprocal child protection agreements with the state of Florida. All that means is that an officer will stop by your relative's home to confirm that Bobby is indeed there, and that he is all right. Remember, that is our only aim here, Mrs. Phillips. We are only interested in answering one basic question: Is Bobby getting proper care, and is he well."

Mom is done talking. She stands up and looks out the tall window. Then she picks up the remote control for the shelf radio, punches it, and the room fills up with graceful music, Mozart or something. Ms. Pagett starts to say something else, but Mom is pushing the volume button. The small radio has a big voice.

The woman police officer comes to the door of the den and talks into Ms. Pagett's ear. Ms. Pagett turns to Mom. She has to shout above the sound of a dozen violins and a harpsichord. "We've concluded our search. Just for the record, Mrs. Phillips, if Bobby is not located and talked to by someone associated with my department within the next five days, then this becomes a police matter. Bobby will be classified as a missing juvenile under suspicious circumstances. You and your husband may be held liable, and in that case you will both face criminal charges. Thank you." Then she turns and leaves.

I know my mom swears once in a while. Like if she burns her hand on a pan, or if her computer freezes when she's trying to print something. But when that social worker and the cops leave the house, Mom cuts loose. The A word? She shouts it. The B word? Mom shakes her fist and hisses that one. She stomps around the first floor of the house, legs stiff, face red, and she works her way through the entire alphabet of swear words, including some stuff I've never heard anyone say before.

Deep down, I guess I always suspected Mom was a real human being. But I didn't know she was *this* real. And I didn't know anyone could get this angry. And I'm glad she's on my side.

When she quiets down, she slumps onto the couch in the TV room and puts her face in her hands, breathing hard. I sit down too, and she feels the couch move. She drops her hands and looks in my direction. She smiles weakly and says, "Sorry I lost my temper. Not very ladylike."

I don't know what to say. I wish she could see me, because then all I'd need to do is nod and smile a little. But I have to say something, so I say, "They deserve it."

Mom shakes her head, "No, they don't, not really, and that's what's so frustrating. These aren't bad people. They're just doing their job, and they sincerely believe that a boy is missing, that something is wrong."

"Well, something *is* wrong—it's just not what they think."

Mom nods. "Right."

"So, what happens now?"

Mom shrugs. "You heard the lady. She said we have five days to show them that our son is alive and well."

"But what if I stay this way and we can't figure it out—I mean, we've already had three weeks! What if five more days isn't enough?"

"Then your dad and I will have to deal with the law."

"Can they arrest you?"

"If they can stomp in here with three police officers and paw through our house, what do you think?"

Before I can answer, Dad comes in the side door and calls, "Em? Bobby?"

"In here, Dad."

First thing, Dad gives Mom a hug, and then takes a long look into her face. "So it was that bad, eh?"

Mom nods. "Yes, it's not good. The case officer's building up evidence that Bobby is missing, and she plans to send someone to Florida to bang on Aunt Ethel's door, and they'll no doubt have a search warrant."

I cut in, "Guys, you know, it might be time to just tell them what's really going on. You haven't done anything wrong. This is my problem, and they're trying to stick the blame on you."

Dad turns his head toward my voice and says, "I know what you're saying, Bobby, and your mom and I appreciate it, but I don't think that's a good idea. If we invite the state to step in, they'll jump in with both feet. The health authorities would have a field day with this. They'd get hold of you, and they'd never let go. They'd categorize your condition, and then just take over— probably treat it as a contagious disease . . . or maybe a disability."

That stops me cold. *I have a disability.* The way I am, it's like being paralyzed or—or blind.

Dad continues. "They'd take you to a hospital or a research facility, and God knows how we'd ever get you back. And I'm not going to let them break up our family."

"But if they arrest my mom and dad, that's breaking

up the family too. And I bet I'd like a research facility a lot more than you'd like the Cook County Jail."

And right away I see I shouldn't have said that, about the Cook County Jail. Because this jolt of fear shoots across their faces, both of them. And it's not like when I was at home alone, feeling afraid of the dark. This is a real threat. The Cook County Jail is a bad place, and I see the fear settle into Dad's eyes, watch it pull at the corners of Mom's mouth.

Looking at their faces, I know I'm not going to let them get arrested and dragged off to jail. That's not going to happen, no matter what. Not to *my* mom and dad.

The lady said we have five whole days. A lot can happen in five days.

It'll have to.

chapter 17

CONNECTIONS

An hour or so after the cops leave, Dad's on his way back to work, and I'm in the kitchen after lunch with Mom, and the phone rings. I pick it up, but before I say a word, Mom grabs the floating receiver out of the air.

"Hello? . . . No, I'm sorry, Bobby isn't here. He's visiting some relatives in Florida, and I'm not sure when he'll be back. I'll tell him to give you a call the next time I talk to him. Good-bye."

She hangs up and turns to me, cold and serious. "Don't answer the phone, Bobby. If Dad isn't around or if I'm not home, just let it ring. Do you understand?"

"Oh. Right, like in case it's that lady calling."

Mom nods. "Or Mrs. Trent, or the school, or just about anybody. You can't use the phone at all, and if you send any e-mails, erase your tracks."

I tilt my head and stare at her in disbelief—which has no effect, because she can't tell I'm doing it. I have no body language. "What . . . like, you think they're going to tap our phones? That's pretty paranoid, Mom."

"Maybe, but maybe not. If I was running this investigation, and I thought a child might be in danger, I'd sure ask a judge for a wiretap, wouldn't you? All I know is, it makes sense to assume the worst."

Which is pretty paranoid, like I said. But I put a shrug

in my voice and say, "Fine. I won't use the phone. Who called?"

"Alicia."

"So, I can't talk to her?" Because I don't think I could stand that.

Mom reaches into her purse and hands me her cell phone. "Use this, and you can give Alicia that number, okay?"

I go up to my room and call Alicia. I'm glad she called, because I've got this idea I want to bounce off her. Except it's a pretty wild idea, and I don't want her to think I'm nuts.

After she answers, she says, "So, how's everything in Florida?" And for a few minutes I forget about my crazy idea because there's plenty of other stuff to talk about.

I say, "Very funny," and I then tell her about the search party. When I'm done, she's not laughing anymore.

"The lady really said your mom and dad could go to jail?"

"No . . . not exactly. But she said there could be criminal prosecution, and that means you get arrested, and when you get arrested, they take you to jail. So it's the same thing."

She's quiet for a few seconds. Then she says, "Guess what book I just finished listening to."

"I don't know . . . something a little lighter than *The Scarlet Letter*, like maybe *Winnie-the-Pooh*? I have no idea."

"*The Invisible Man*, by H. G. Wells."

"Oh. And you're reading this because of me, right?"

"Of course."

"I'm deeply honored. So, how is it?"

"Creepy. I think H. G. Wells has some serious issues. All his books are about wackos who try to take over the world. This character he made up is a real nutcase. But the part about how the man made himself disappear is pretty interesting. You should read it."

"I'd rather have you give me a summary."

"Because you're lazy?"

"Right, and because it's hard for me to check books out of the library right now."

"Okay. Fine. So this half-crazy albino guy feels like a freak, but he's also kind of a genius, and he starts studying light, the way light works. And he gets this idea that if he could make every part of his body reflect light the same way that air does—which is not at all—then his whole body would be as invisible as air, and he could be completely transparent and have all this power. For him, it's all about the power. And he mixes up all these chemicals that can change the way his body reflects light, and he drinks this humongous drug cocktail, and he feels like he's going to die, and he passes out, and when he wakes up, his body has disappeared. At first he's happy, but what he finds out is that being invisible is terrible and that all these ignorant people are scared to death of him, and that makes him even crazier, and he turns into this schizoid homicidal maniac, and at the end it takes about six men to finally kill him."

She pauses, and I don't say anything.

"Bobby?"

"So, that's the story?"

"You said you wanted a summary."

"This sounds like a book I really need right now. Discouraging and disturbing, yet also deeply depressing. Thanks so much for sharing. Maybe you should start Alicia's Book Club. Here's your slogan: 'Books to Push You Over the Edge.' "

She doesn't say anything. So I say, "Sorry. Still, you have to admit, that's a pretty depressing story."

"But it's not, it's *not* depressing!" I can picture her face, and her intensity surprises me. "Because when I was listening to this book, all I could think of was that *you* are nothing like this guy. You aren't some crazy person trying to prove some big point, or become a famous scientist or something. You were nice before this happened, and you're still a good person. It's not like you wanted any of this. It's just an accident. You're innocent, and this other guy's guilty. Plus, he doesn't trust anybody. And that's not like you. This guy is all on his own because he's so selfish. You're not alone like he was. Like, your mom and dad? They would go to jail just to keep you safe. You have people who care about you and want to protect you."

"People like you?" That stops her.

". . . Well . . . yeah."

Now she's blushing, I'm sure of it. I say, "You've really thought about all this, haven't you?"

"In case you haven't noticed, Bobby, I really think about everything. Just because I'm blind doesn't mean I'm stupid."

Her sarcasm doesn't bother me anymore. Besides, it's my fault for getting personal. So I say, "I think you're right about this being an accident. But my dad says there's no such thing as an accident. He says there's only cause and effect. So anyway, I got this strange idea this morning, and I want to know if you think it's stupid, okay?"

"Sure."

"You know how when something bad happens, everybody says, 'Of all the people in the world, how come this had to happen to me?' Well, I'm lying on my bed early this morning reading an article in *Time* magazine about people who have had UFO abduction experiences. And I read that until the media got going on this, all these people—hundreds of them—they all kept quiet about it because they thought it only happened to them. And I look at myself, at all this, and I think, What makes you so sure this is only happening to you? Maybe going invisible has happened to other people too. Maybe lots of people! And everybody is keeping it a secret and thinks he's the only one in the world with this problem."

Alicia says, "So you're saying . . . maybe there's this whole squad of other invisible people out there some-where? . . . That's pretty hard to believe."

"Is five invisible people harder to believe than just one? Is five or ten or a hundred any weirder than one? Okay, think about this: Do you and your dad ever talk about life in outer space?"

Alicia snorts. "Are you kidding? My dad's a nut about

that. He says because there's life here on Earth, there *must* be life other places in the universe too. The universe is so huge, he says it's stupid to think that Earth is the only place with intelligent life."

"Exactly. Because the same things that caused life here probably caused it to happen somewhere else, right? So here I am, and I've gone invisible without trying to, and something had to cause it, and maybe the same causes did it to someone else as well. Like life on some other planet. It's not so crazy." I'm trying not to sound too excited about this, but I am.

Alicia's not going to just go along with it, though. She says, "Well, maybe it's not crazy, but so what? Let's say you could actually find someone else who's invisible, then what? What good does that do?"

"It's good because then we could compare notes, that's why. That's why when scientists do experiments, they do them lots of times—to compare the results." I stop and think a second because I want her to see why this could be important. Then I say, "Okay, when you lost your sight, did the doctors ever talk about other cases—cases like yours?"

Now she's thinking. "Yeah—actually, that was the first thing they did! They looked through this huge database of other patients, scanning for people with the same kind of problems and conditions as mine. They wanted to see what the best treatment would be."

"Exactly. And did they find any cases like yours?"

"About fifty, and that was just in North America."

"Did it help?"

". . . Kind of. It confirmed what they already thought. People with my kind of problem can't be helped."

"Oh." And I remember that information can cut both ways.

"But that doesn't mean it would be the same for you, Bobby. If we found just one other person, then we compare both cases, and if details start matching up, then you've got some real clues, right?"

"Right," I say, "but that's where I hit a brick wall. Because if there are others like me, how do we find them? Like, run an ad in the newspaper? 'Having Problems With Invisibility? Call Bobby, and say so long to your troubles.' "

Alicia giggles. "You'd probably get some very strange replies."

"Right. That's the brick wall. Because even if there *was* some other person like me, and even if we could find him, what good would it do? Because the cops are still gonna crash in here five days from now and try to arrest my parents."

"But it's something to work on, Bobby, and it's not like you've got some other big plan, right? And you can't just sit around and feel sorry for yourself, do nothing for five days—right?"

It's her tone that gets to me. "Who said anything about doing nothing? That's what drives me nuts about talking to you sometimes. You twist everything around and run it through a grinder, and then shoot it back at me."

"Sorry you're so sensitive. You brought it up, as I recall—all these invisible people running around the world, right? You asked me, I said it sounded like something worth looking into, and then *you* turn around and say it's all just pointless."

"I didn't say it's all pointless. I just have trouble seeing how it makes sense to start hunting around for other invisible people, that's all."

"So what *does* make sense to you, Bobby?"

"Right now? Nothing makes any sense at all."

Now she's pushing. "Oh, come on. Don't do the 'poor little Bobby' routine. Let's get this thing figured out. What are some other ideas? There must be some other ideas, right?"

"No. I really don't have any other ideas. Believe it or not, I just wanted to talk things out a little, you know, talk to a friend. Remember friends, Alicia? Friends are people who—"

"Yeah," she snaps, "yeah, I remember. Don't you start lecturing me. Don't even think about it, Bobby. I've got to go now, and you? You've got to find someone else who wants to sit around and listen to you snivel about everything. Let me know how it all works out, Bobby."

"Sure. You bet. Go ahead and hang up. Good-bye."

I hold the phone on my ear, waiting for her to hang up. She doesn't. I can hear her breathing.

"Hey—Alicia."

"What?"

"Thought you had to go."

"I thought you said good-bye."

"But then you didn't hang up."

"Neither did you."

"Look, Alicia, I know that idea's crazy. Or maybe it's actually a good idea—it's practically the only one I've had so far. I just don't know what to think about anything, that's all. So I'll keep thinking, okay? I'll think about that, I'll think about everything. There has to be something, some idea. Because if there's not, then I might just walk into that lady's office at Child and Family Services tomorrow and plant my butt on her desk and tell her I'm fine, and let her hold my invisible hand and take my pulse. I'll get right up in her face and make her deal with the facts of the case, and just see what happens. Or maybe I'll make her an offer she can't refuse, maybe haunt her office all day, trash her computer, help her forget about me. Maybe visit her house a couple nights in a row, maybe scare her to death. Or maybe I'll write a juicy suicide note and set things up so my mom and dad are in the clear, and then I can go to my own funeral like Huck Finn did. And then just disappear. I don't know—I just don't know."

When I'm done talking, Alicia doesn't say anything. All I hear is breathing. And when she talks, it's her small voice.

"I know where you are right now, Bobby. I've been there too. I have. And if it hadn't been for Nancy, I'd have probably tried to kill myself or done something else really stupid, stuff like you're talking about. So I'm going to be your Nancy. I'm not giving up on you, no matter how long it takes for things to get better, or even if things never do get better. And even if you give up on yourself, I'm not giving up on you. And I don't believe you're going to get mean or go crazy or any of that. I just don't believe it, Bobby. I know better."

I don't know what to say. But I don't want to stop talking either.

After about five seconds Alicia says, "Bobby?"

"Yes?"

"Let's hang up now, okay? But you can call me back anytime. Or we can get together, like maybe go for a walk. Or whatever, okay? Anytime."

"Okay."

"And don't do anything crazy, all right?"

"I won't."

"Promise?"

"Yeah, I promise."

"Good. Talk to you later, Bobby."

"Okay. Good-bye."

We both hang up, but it's like there's still a connection. I can feel it.

And it feels good.

chapter 18
PIZZA AND PUZZLES

T he dinner is Dad's idea. He calls from work late
Monday afternoon and tells Mom that he called
Alicia's dad and invited their family to come for
pizza at 7:30. Mom squawks, but it's already set up, so
we're having a dinner party.

Except it's not really a dinner party. It's a meeting.
About me. The dads finally want to talk deep science
about the Bobby situation, and the rest of us will have to
make the best of it.

When sets of parents get together, it's always risky
for the kids. Back at the beginning of fourth grade I had
this friend named Ted. We had fun messing around at
school, and he came to my house for an overnight once.

Then Mom got the bright idea that his family should
come for dinner. Ted's parents were nice people, just not
educated like Mom and Dad. Ted's dad ran the parts department at a Ford dealership, and his mom was the sec-
retary at a real estate agency.

It was a bad night. Mom wore a black dress and pearls,
and she cooked this fancy meal. Dad wore a sport coat
and tie, and he was icing down some expensive wine
when the doorbell rang. Ted's folks walked in wearing
jeans and matching Disney World T-shirts, and they
handed Dad a cold six-pack of Miller Light to help the
party along.

And that night pretty much ruined my friendship with Ted.

But tonight's different. Tonight is more like a science seminar, and under the circumstances, everybody seems pretty comfortable.

Except maybe for Mrs. Van Dorn. She doesn't really want to be here. I think she wishes I'd never bumped into Alicia. She shakes Mom's hand, and they look like they can survive the evening together, but I don't see a great friendship in their future.

Mrs. Van Dorn is only a little taller than Alicia, so Mom makes her look tiny. She's got narrow shoulders and slender arms with delicate wrists, graceful hands with long, thin fingers. She's not as pretty as Alicia, but she might have been, about twenty-five years ago. Her hair is longer than Alicia's and she pulls it back from her face with a comb on each side. It's about the same shade of brown. There's a strength in the way she carries herself, but she never seems to relax, never lets down her guard.

Alicia seems so much more self-confident than her mom. And I think Alicia must get some of that from her dad. Because the professor is way off in his own orbit—out where it doesn't matter how crazy your hair looks. The U of C has a killer astronomy department, and this guy is way out on the front edge. He's only in the door three seconds before he starts spouting some theory about spectral analysis and the refractive indices of protein substances, and he's carrying a big box full of books and papers. Dad nods as the professor talks, and then he flips out some chunks of jargon, and all the while they're both peering at the well-dressed young man who's got no hands or head poking out of his flannel shirt—which is me. I'm thinking it's going to be a long night, and the slightly embarrassed look on Alicia's face tells me she agrees.

Still, it's hard to ruin pizza and root beer and ice cream, and once the eating starts, things loosen up. During dinner everyone is careful not to talk about Bobby the missing person—or the cops, or jail time—so there's nothing to do but chat and try to be happy.

Mom and Mrs. Van Dorn—who has now become Julia—discover that they both went to Northwestern and both majored in English literature. So they're in academic heaven, talking about this professor and that course, this novel and that poem, and all of a sudden I'm afraid that they might turn into good friends after all. Because I bet that having moms be pals is almost as tough on kids as having moms who can't stand each other.

So after dinner the dads are in the front parlor with the French doors closed, leaning over a big round table, each scribbling away on pads of yellow paper, spinning out theories like madmen. Dad has his collection of books and articles spread out on a card table within easy reach. I look through the glass door, and I can see my file folder there on the corner of the card table, my time line, and the lists of stuff in my room. It looks like they've got a long night ahead of them.

Alicia and I are sitting on the floor at the living room

coffee table, and we're done with our pizza. The moms are sitting on the couch, jumping up every few minutes to pull a favorite book off the shelves, laughing and impressing each other with their deep mutual love of literature.

And I whisper to Alicia, "Let's go online, okay?" And she nods, as eager to escape as I am.

Mom glances at me as we stand up. She reads my mind—which is something she's too good at—and says, "Remember, Bobby, if you send any e-mail, erase your tracks from the hard disk when you're done."

It's a lot quieter in the study. I help Alicia to a chair beside the desk. The computer starts humming, and I ask, "Do you use the Net much? It's pretty visual."

Alicia pulls her legs up under her on the chair. "I've got some pretty good voice and text software, and I'm going to learn how to use those Braille readers. But sites like National Public Radio and news sites have a lot of audio. Plus music sites. But when I need to get information, I usually need a guide. At the library I can get a reference assistant. And as a last resort, my mom'll always help."

"Last resort, huh?"

"*Very* last."

"Does your mom work?"

Alicia makes a face. "Yeah. She works on me. *I'm* her big job. She used to work for a public relations company, did a lot of traveling to New York and LA. Now she does a little writing and a little consulting and a lot of looking after Alicia. Unexpected career change. If I get independent enough, she can go back to work without feeling guilty all the time. That's my big goal. Then maybe I can stop feeling guilty about ruining her life."

I feel like I should say something more, but I don't want her to get mad. And she's already in a half-rotten mood.

So I say, "I've got a search engine open. Pick a topic."

"That's easy. Type 'invisible people.' "

I plug it in and hit return. "Jeez! You're not going to believe this!"

Alicia leans forward in her chair. "Try me."

"The search 'invisible people' hits on 450,623 pages!"

"No way! Read me some."

"Okay. Here's the first one: The Invisible People Club. It's a joke site. They've got a picture here with a list of gag names, and the picture frame is empty. Big yuks. Then there's one—more like ten pages—about a tribe in Brazil called the Invisible People. . . . Here's some stuff about women's rights . . . the homeless . . . street people . . . a rock group called Invisible People, some comic books . . . CIA spies, computer privacy . . . now I'm jumping ahead about six screen loads, and . . . and there's stuff about UFOs, Eastern religion . . . and so on and so on and so on. Endless. And weird."

"How about if you just search for 'invisibility.' "

"Okay . . . here we are. Invisibility. . . . Fewer pages, but still a lot, like, over a hundred and eight thousand. And more interesting stuff. Here's one about scientists in Texas who are injecting fluids into rats to see if they can make skin transparent so they can do the same to people one day. They want to look at your guts without cutting you open. Nice. And it works, except the stuff they use might be poison."

"And that's not a joke?"

"Very real. There are newspaper articles and everything. Then . . . there's the Stealth Bomber . . . ancient Hindu spells, reincarnation . . . Internet shopping privacy issues . . . more comic books . . . spiritualism. Here's a page called The Invisibility of God, and tons about ghosts . . . alien abductions . . . all kinds of stuff. . . . Whoa!"

"What?"

"This site is called Human Spontaneous Involuntary Invisibility . . . it's an essay by a lady, and she's serious. . . . She says she's talked with a lot of people who apparently just stopped being visible to others around them, sometimes for a few minutes, sometimes longer . . . and other people can't see them or hear them. That's so *weird*."

Alicia giggles. "Look who's talking."

"Right. But this stuff is all, like . . . mystical. What we were talking about on the phone today? I was talking about reality, real people, not a bunch of hocus-pocus."

"And what makes you so sure that science is so reliable? Or that the university crowd has any better answers than the hocus-pocus gang?"

"Me? Sure? I'm not sure about anything. I'm just saying that this stuff I'm reading about here is all chat, it's people telling this lady what happened to them, and then she writes about it, and wonders out loud. She's not saying she ever actually saw anyone in that condition. Like my dad, the scientist, says when he points at me, 'This is an event!' I'm right here, and my matter isn't reflecting or refracting any light. What's happening to me isn't hearsay or rumor or theory. So I guess that's why I'm not into the abracdabra scene. I'm an event." And out of the corner of my ear I hear myself. I'm being very logical. Like Dad. Pretty scary.

And the logic is working, because Alicia's agreeing with me. "So apparently no one else who's had an event like yours is advertising it on the Net tonight."

"That's the way it looks. But invisibility is an idea that's out there in a big way. People are into this. This hypnotist, the one who's writing about these people who claim they've gone invisible? She says people have been working at becoming invisible since about 700 B.C. Listen to this from some ancient writer in India: '. . . concentration and meditation can make the body imperceptible to other men, and "a direct contact with the light of the eyes no longer existing, the body disappears." ' That's what's happening to me, except I didn't sit around chanting or praying. I just went to bed, and when I got up, all gone."

The computer keeps humming and the two of us sit there, silently thinking. Thinking together.

"Bobby?! Emily!" It's Dad, yelling.

Dad's tone of voice makes us all rush for the parlor. Mom and Mrs. Van Dorn get to the front of the house before Alicia and I do.

Dad's on his feet, pacing, and when Alicia and I get there, he stops and looks at me.

"I feel really stupid, Bobby. I didn't pay enough attention to the information about your room. And then five minutes ago I mention it to Leo, and he takes one look at your data charts, and bingo!—he hits on something!" Dad's beaming at me, but he's too excited to stop for more than a second. He turns to Mom. "Now, Emily, I'd like you and Julia to go up to Bobby's room and get his electric blanket, the blanket itself, and the controller and all the wires. And don't bang the controller or drop it, all right? And Bobby, I want you to go down to the basement and find my old oscilloscope. Leo and I will try to find something else we need, which I think is in the kitchen. Okay? Let's go!"

And everyone scatters for the treasure hunt.

Find Dad's old oscilloscope. That's not a job. It's more like a career. Because of our basement. Alicia follows me halfway down the stairs.

"You'd better stop there," I say, and she does. "Okay, the oscilloscope is a boxy thing about as big as a small suitcase. Has a round green screen on one end, and there are wires and knobs and switches all over it. In most basements, not a problem to find. Down here, big problem. This basement is the kind of place archaeologists dream about. I'm looking at a twenty-year history of the technological revolution in America."

Alicia sits down on the steps. "What do you mean?"

"I mean, our basement is a high-tech junkyard because my dad can't bear to throw anything away, espe-cially not something electronic. That's because, if you're smart enough, you can look at anything and think of twenty or thirty possible ways that it might be useful at some point in the future, so you just keep it."

Now I'm picking my way around the heaps and piles and sagging shelves. I look around and I see about twelve different generations of CPUs, three or four black-and-white monitors, two old color monitors, an original Macintosh, six different computer game systems, an an-cient tube radio, a little box of broken Walkman tape players and radios, three fax machines, a bin of outdated telephones and cell phones and beepers, and four TVs. And hiding here behind the shipping box for an ancient IBM wheel printer—the oscilloscope.

"Got it!" It's heavy, and as I move to the stairs with it, Alicia gets to her feet, and I follow her up to the kitchen.

Dad and Leo are pawing through a mound of paper on the breakfast table, the contents of three or four fat fold-ers from the cabinet above the wall oven. That's where Dad sticks the information sheets and the instruction booklets and the warranty information whenever we buy something. So there are instruction manuals in there for everything from the garbage disposal to the new ink-jet printer to the bike I got for Christmas when I was seven.

And Leo grabs something and holds it up. "This is it!"

It's the information that came with my electric blan-ket when it was new.

Leo's excited now, flipping through the stapled pages. ". . . And we're in luck! Here's the schematic diagram!"

Alicia makes a face. "What's that?"

Dad's looking over Leo's shoulder, and he says, "The schematic diagram shows the electrical details—it's like a map of how the electricity flows, and it shows imped-ance and resistance, the voltage at different points, any motors or capacitors, transformers or resistors, things like that." One of Dad's degrees is in electrical engi-neering.

Alicia nods, and I can tell from her face that she's into the spirit of the hunt, tilting her head to listen as Dad starts rooting through the kitchen junk drawer.

With a little "Aha!" he grabs a small screwdriver set and says, "I think we have everything now."

Then Mom and Mrs. Van Dorn come down the back stairs with the blanket, and we all follow Dad back to the front parlor, me still lugging the oscilloscope.

Alicia's father studies the diagram while Dad un-screws the metal bottom of the blanket controller. He looks up and says, "Em, would you plug in the scope?" So I help Mom get the cover off the oscilloscope and find the power cord.

Mrs. Van Dorn says, "What are you looking for, Leo?"

Her husband glances up from the diagram. "Flaws. We want to see if this controller unit is working right. Because if it's not, it could be generating an unusual field."

"A field?"

He looks back at the diagram, nodding. "Electric blankets always create an electron field of some sort, because you can't run power through ten or twelve yards of wire without causing an electromagnetic disturbance. The question is, what kind of disturbance, and what magnitude?"

Mrs. Van Dorn nods, and I can't tell from her face if she followed all that or not.

Dad's got the screws out and lifts the metal bottom off the blanket controller. Then he picks up two probes hooked onto wires coming from the front of the oscilloscope, a red one and a black one. He fiddles with a dial and flips some switches, pokes the pointers down into the guts of the controller, looks at the scope, looks at the diagram, frowns, and then touches something else. Except for the hum of the green cathode tube, it's quiet.

Alicia says, "What's going on?"

I whisper, "My dad's poking around with these wires that are hooked to the machine I found in the basement. He's testing the electrical parts of my electric blanket control." I see Alicia's fingers tremble, sensing the tension in the room. Dad yelps and we both jump.

"Ha!" Dad is pointing at the screen. "See that?"

Leo squints. "What?"

"This resistor is way outside its parameters. It's letting about six times too much power through!"

Mom says, "What's it mean?"

"Not sure yet. Bobby, have you noticed this blanket being hotter than normal?"

"Nope. Works same as always."

"Hmm." Dad makes a note on the sheet, then starts poking around again.

"Dad?" I'm speaking softly.

"Umm . . . yes?" Dad's looking at the diagram every few seconds.

"So . . . you're checking every part? Like, to see what's not working?"

Dad doesn't answer until he makes another note. ". . . Yes, looking for anything unusual."

I turn to Dr. Van Dorn. "And when you saw the blanket on my list, was it, like, the idea of force fields just jumped out at you?"

Alicia's dad nods, his lips pressed tightly together. His eyes don't leave the diagram, and he taps the sheet and says, "Get a reading on this rheostat, David. If the dial's out of alignment, that could double or triple the current getting past."

Dad shakes his head. "I want to check the throughput reactance first."

I say, "Reactance? Is that like resistance?"

Dad shakes his head. "Different principle."

Then I get an idea. "Hey, Dr. Van Dorn—should we check out the other stuff on my nightstand? There's an old phone, and a digital alarm clock too. I mean, they sit right there on the table, right next to the blanket controller. Do you think maybe they're throwing off electrical fields too? Like maybe they're affecting the blanket controller? I could run upstairs and get them— Dad, do you think we should test them too?"

Neither of them answer me.

I look at Dad. He squints and touches the probes to a different pair of contacts inside the controller. He glances at the diagram and says, "Leo? Take a look at the value for that third resistor—is that a two or a five?"

Alicia's dad bends closer to the schematic. "Five. Definitely." So Dad nods and moves the probes again.

He's forgotten I'm in the room. Dad's off in science land with his pal the professor.

I feel my face getting hot, feel my jaw muscles tighten. I clench my teeth, biting back the anger. Because inside my head, I'm yelling at them, at both of them. *Hey! Excuse me . . . WHO had the idea that the answer wasn't off in theoryville, that the place to begin was at the scene of the crime? What's that? That was MY idea? Well, what do you know! And guess what? If you'd talk and LISTEN, maybe I have other ideas too. Or does that sound like science fiction to such big geniuses?*

A minute goes by, and I've got myself back under control. I'm not shouting in my head now, but I'm thinking, *Who needs this? I'm supposed to just stand around and be part of their audience? I don't think so.*

I glance at Alicia. She's not having such a great time either.

So I say, "Hey, Alicia, wanna get some more ice cream? They'll let us know if anything exciting happens, right, Dad?" I see Alicia's smile flicker when I say that. Alicia understands sarcasm, even the subtle kind.

Dad doesn't know I've made a little joke. He nods distractedly and says, "Sure . . . you bet."

So we leave the science guys in the parlor with no one but their adoring wives to cheer them on.

I yank open the freezer. "Mint chocolate chip or black raspberry?"

Alicia wrinkles her nose. "How about you count to ten and then ask me again—without snarling."

I laugh, but only a little. "Okay. How's this: Miss, would you prefer mint chocolate chip or black raspberry?"

Alicia pretends to flirt with me. She bats her eyelashes, tilts her head, and says, "Which do *you* prefer?"

"Definitely the raspberry."

She smiles and says, "Then I'll have mint chocolate chip so you can have an extra-big dish of your favorite."

By the time we get to the couch in the family room, I'm cured. I can get back to being mad some other time. Right now, I'm just glad to be with Alicia.

I hit the remote and start flipping through the channels. When I get to AMC, Alicia says, "Stop there! I love this movie!"

It's *The King and I*, the original one with the bald guy and all the singing and dancing.

I watch and Alicia listens, and then I ask, "What's it like, just hearing it?"

"Better than you'd think. But that's because I used to love this movie when I was little. I watched it about twenty times. I'm in replay mode."

"So, do you see it in color?"

"Yup. And I can see the lady's dresses, and the little things the kids wear up on the top of their heads, the whole thing. I mean, I see what I can remember, and I probably add stuff of my own. And when they almost kiss, that part gets me—I always wished the king would just grab her and give her a big kiss."

"How about other movies, ones you haven't seen?"

She shakes her head. "It's not so bad if I have an idea what the story's about. It's like a radio play with music that's too loud. When I can listen to a movie I've seen, that's the best. Like *Titanic*. I can see the whole thing. But for new stories, now I like books better. Then I get to make up the movie in my head. And it's weird, about people I saw in movies a couple of years ago? Like, I'm never going to see Brad Pitt get old. He's stuck in my mind from about three years ago. He could keep acting till he's eighty, but when I listen to a Brad Pitt movie, I'm always going to see him as the little brother from *A River Runs Through It*. Don't you think that's neat?"

She puts a last spoonful of ice cream in her mouth.

"Yeah, I guess."

Alicia's quiet a minute, and I watch her face. It's the part of the movie where the kids are putting on the play of *Uncle Tom's Cabin*. And I'm wondering what she really sees. There's this peaceful smile on her lips, and I think that maybe it's like she's in the movie herself, now sitting at the dinner table, now running around on the stage with the kids. I don't think I could ever get tired of watching her face.

She shifts expression and tilts her face toward me. "You're staring at me, aren't you?"

I feel myself blush. "No."

"Liar. It's okay. I don't mind having you stare."

I gulp. I don't know what to say, but I don't want to sound flustered, so I say, "Another question: What do you see when you think of me? What do I look like in your mind? . . . Brad Pitt?"

Now she's blushing too, a shy smile pulling at the corners of her mouth. "I don't know. I know you're taller than I am. I know you have a nice smile—because I can hear a smile. It's something you can't fake. But I don't know. I mean, like, I don't know if your nose is big or not, I don't know if you've got brown hair or blond hair, stuff like that." She pauses. "And I guess it doesn't matter. I really haven't been thinking about how you might look. It's more like . . . a feeling I have about you. I know you're honest, and smart. And kind, at least most of the time."

"Don't forget loyal and trustworthy—you've got me sounding like the perfect Boy Scout." I'm choosing words carefully. "But . . . don't you wonder what would've happened if you hadn't been blind, and I was my regular self, and we just met somewhere—like that day at the library, except we were both just high school kids?"

"What do you think?"

"I don't know. You said you were pretty popular before. The popular kids at my school don't even know I'm alive."

"How come?"

"Because I'm just average, and they're all good looking or rich, or both, or super athletes or something."

"Do you really think you're average? I'd never think that, not after getting to know you."

"But that's what I mean. At school you'd have never gotten to know me. I'm one of those kids you wouldn't have looked at twice. I'd just be this idiot who bashes into you at the door of the library one day, and all your popular friends would point and say, 'Hey—way to go, dorkness!' "

The movie is loud, a full orchestra playing while Anna and the king of Siam twirl around and around a wide, shiny floor. But Alicia is facing me, a foot away, and I can't tell what she's thinking. And I don't know if I should be talking to her this way.

"But you're judging them at the same time you accuse them of judging you. It's like you've got a prejudice against the popular kids, and you assume they have a bad attitude toward you."

"I'm not assuming anything. I'm talking about experience. You can tell if someone thinks you're nothing. Like, just a few weeks ago, I'm walking toward this beautiful girl named Jessica in the hall, and I smile and look at her, and her face doesn't change, her eyes don't connect with me, nothing. It's like she looks right through me, like I'm not even there."

Alicia's eyebrows shoot up. "Hmm . . . she looked right through you, eh? Like you weren't even there?

Interesting way to describe your old life, don't you think?"

In the movie, the young girl who's run away from the palace has been captured, and now she's on her knees before the king, waiting for her death sentence.

I see what Alicia's saying, but I'm not going to get sucked into some stupid psychobabble session. So I just clam up, sit back, and look at the TV.

Alicia senses I've turned away, so she lets the conversation drop.

We're still sitting there twenty minutes later when her mom comes in.

"Alicia? Time to go now."

Alicia stands up and takes her mom's elbow. "Did they get the blanket figured out?"

I tense up because that's an important question right now. Mrs. Van Dorn pauses. It's just a half second, but that pause tells me everything.

She says, "I'm not sure. You'll have to ask your dad about that. Bobby, it was nice to visit. You have a lovely home . . . and I'm sure everything is going to work out all right for you."

I'm standing too, facing Mrs. Van Dorn. I say, "Thanks," but I don't mean it. I don't mean it because I don't believe what she said—that "everything is going to work out all right." That's just something parents say. It's something they say at bedtime so you won't lie awake worrying all night like they do. They *hope* things will work out okay, and they might even *believe* things will be all right in the end, but are they sure, really sure? And when I look at Dad's face and see the strained way he shakes hands and says good night to Alicia's dad, I know I'm right. No one knows anything. It's all guesswork.

When they're gone, Mom starts bustling around, cleaning up and taking glasses into the kitchen, all bright and cheery. "Wasn't this a lovely evening? They are such nice people. I can't get over how Julia was at Northwestern—you know, we only missed each other by two years. And she took some of my favorite courses, same professors, same lecture halls—David, I should have you calculate the chances of meeting someone like that. Do you know she even took that course on Rilke that I loved so much, the one about the *Duino Elegies*? I bet the chances of finding someone like that are a million to one, maybe more, don't you think?"

Dad's not talking. He's nodding, and he's trying to smile, and he's pitching in with the cleanup, but he's still working. Working on the Bobby puzzle.

I'm at his elbow at the sink, handing him plates to scrape and rinse. And I say, "So, tell me all about the blanket, Dad."

Dad keeps busy with the dish brush. "Nothing to tell. Leo's got a few other ideas, but basically, we ran out of science. Sort of hit a theoretical dead end." He pauses and looks my way. "But, you know, you did a good job— the way you approached that data collection. Good clear thinking, Bobby."

162

"Thanks. So, did you get any other ideas? Any break-throughs?"

He focuses on the dish brush, swishing the suds around, trying to get a streak of pizza cheese off a plate without getting his cast wet. I can tell that holding the plate puts a strain on his broken wrist. "Wish I had good news, Bobby, but I don't, not tonight."

And that's all he says. He doesn't try to sugarcoat it for me. He doesn't say, "But, you know, son, I'm sure everything's gonna be just fine in the end."

And later when I'm thinking about what Dad said and the way he said it, I tell myself that I appreciate his honesty. And I tell myself that Dad knows I'm not a little kid anymore, that he knows I'm mature enough to face facts. And I tell myself that in real life, things get messed up, and sometimes they stay that way. And I tell myself I'm proud of myself for being so mentally strong, so tough-minded.

But what I focus on as I head down toward sleep is what Mom says when she tucks me in. Because she says what I want to believe.

"Now, don't worry, Bobby. You get a good night's rest. I just know that everything's going to be fine."

chapter 19
GENERAL BOBBY

I don't have a good night's rest. I miss my electric blanket. The down quilt Mom put on my bed is too light, and it keeps slipping off during the night. And off and on, all night long, I keep thinking about my electric blanket. It's definitely faulty. It definitely puts out an energy field. And I definitely spent the last seven hours of my life as a normal person tucked underneath it.

After I finally do get some sleep, I wake up Tuesday morning with a new idea—make that a huge idea, an amazing idea. Because if my condition *did* have anything to do with a bad electric blanket, there must be a lot of other people who bought that same electric blanket. Probably thousands. And if you get a bad blanket, you send it back. You complain to the manufacturer. There could have been a product recall. There would be records. And if there are records, then there are names. Names of people. And it's just possible that any one of those people could be . . . like me.

Dad's already gone by the time I get up. Mom says he stayed up late, running different tests, writing down results. Then he left for the lab early. "And he said not to disturb anything in the parlor." So Dad hasn't really given up on the blanket either. Still, even if he was home now, I'm not sure I'd talk to him about my idea.

Mom leaves to get ready for her ten o'clock Introduction to Literature class, and I grab a pen and paper and go to the parlor the minute she's gone. I thought maybe Dad had taken the information sheets about the blanket to work with him, but they're on the piano bench. The fronts and backs of all four sheets are covered with Dad's tiny, precise handwriting. But I'm not interested in any of that. I don't need to formulate a workable theory. All I need is the model number and the manufacturer. It takes less than ten seconds to jot down.

My blanket is a twin-size, single-control, Dyna-Rest Supreme electric blanket, model DRS-T-1349-7A. The faded sticker on the metal bottom of the controller unit has the same numbers. And the blanket is unconditionally guaranteed for a period of three years by Sears, Roebuck and Company, Chicago, Illinois.

On my way into the den, I do the math. The blanket isn't under warranty. Mom got me this blanket the first day we moved here from Houston, which was in March of my fifth-grade year. I remember the day exactly—cold and windy, no azaleas in bloom, no heated swimming pool in the backyard.

Sears. You can't live in Chicago without knowing where Sears is. Sears Tower is the tallest thing in the city, and for a long time it was the tallest building in the world.

And you think if you know where the Sears Tower is, you know where Sears is. Wrong. That's an illusion. Because I do a little Internet search and learn that Sears moved their company offices out to the suburbs years ago, about thirty-five miles west—so far away, they can't even see their huge tower. I pick up the phone and start to dial the main number, and then I remember. I hang up, go to my room, get Mom's cell phone, carry it to the den, and dial again.

"Thank you for calling Sears. This calling menu has changed, so please listen carefully. If you know the five digit extension of the party you are trying to reach . . ."

And the recording goes on for about three minutes. I work my way through the menus and get to the consumer merchandise customer service line. Then I have to slog through nine choices until finally I'm asked to hold for the next available customer service representative.

After fourteen minutes and a lot of bad music, a voice says, "Hello, this is Renee. May I help you?"

I try to sound as grown-up as possible, because nobody at any company ever wants to talk to a kid about anything. "Yes, Renee, I'm calling about a possible problem with my electric blanket."

"Yes, sir. But first, may I have your name and telephone number?"

So I give her Dad's name and the home number, and then she wants our Sears charge account number. "I don't have the card with me at the moment, because all I really want is some information."

"Yes, sir? I will be happy to give you information about your Sears product. May I have the name and the model number, please?"

I give her the information, and while she's tapping away on a keyboard, I say, "I need to know if there's been a problem with this blanket."

"Are you experiencing a difficulty in using or maintaining your Sears product, sir?"

This is tricky. "Well, I'm not sure. It might be acting a little strange."

"Do you use a heart pacemaker, sir?"

"A what?"

"A heart pacemaker, sir."

"No. I . . . I just want to know if there have been any problems with this particular blanket."

"Sir, the notes I have for this product show that we are encouraging any customer who has this item to send it to our customer service center and receive a comparable product of equal or greater value in exchange. Any person using a heart pacemaker should be encouraged not to use this product. And Sears will pay the shipping and handling fees for the exchange. Would you like me to go ahead and schedule a UPS pickup, sir?"

"Can you tell me how many of these blankets have been returned?"

"I do not have that information, sir. We are encouraging any customer who has this item to send it to our customer service center and receive a comparable product of equal or greater value in exchange. And Sears will pay the shipping and handling fees. Would you like me to go ahead and schedule the UPS pickup, sir?"

"Does anyone have a record of who has returned this product to Sears?"

"I don't know anything about that, sir. But you can return that model number for a product of equal or greater value. Would you like me to go ahead and schedule a UPS pickup for your blanket, sir?"

"No. No, thanks. Good-bye."

"Good-bye, sir, and thank you for calling Sears Customer Service."

My next call is Alicia.

"Guess what?"

"Um . . . you woke up this morning perfectly normal, and you've also figured out what's wrong with my eyes."

"Nice guess. But you know my electric blanket? It's made by Sears, and when I called customer service just now and asked about this model, the lady told me that anyone who calls about it is supposed to send it back for a free replacement. And the lady asked me if I use a heart pacemaker, because the note in the file says to tell anyone with a pacemaker not to use it."

Alicia says, "So . . . that means something's seriously wrong with your blanket. How many've been returned?"

"Don't know. But if they're offering to replace it, a lot of people must have had trouble with it."

"So can we talk to some of them? You get any names?"

"No numbers, no names. That's why I called you. Who should I call next?"

Alicia doesn't hesitate a second. "Definitely the legal department. My mom used to do public relations for big companies, and sometimes she had to do damage control. That's what she called it. You know, a company has a bad product, and they fix it, and then they have to do a media campaign to make sure people know everything's all fixed. But the lawyers are always in the middle of it. So you call the legal department, and you tell them you've got a question about product liability. Mom says that makes big companies crazy. You know, like when all those tires went bad on SUVs? That's why big companies hire jillions of lawyers. You say, 'This is David So-and-so from the product liability research center in Baltimore or somewhere, and we've gotten a report that such-and-such a blanket is malfunctioning.' Something like that, just make it up. And see if you can get somebody to tell you how many claims they've had, who keeps the records, all that stuff."

I gulp. "I couldn't do that. They'd never believe me . . . but how about this? How about I read you the phone number for Sears and *you* call them? You sound like you know what you're talking about . . . and I think you're a better actor than I am."

"You think I'm a better actor? What does that mean? You think I'm a good liar, is that it?"

"Jeez—touchy, touchy. It's a compliment. I mean you could probably sound like you know something, and I'm just gonna to sound like this dumb kid, that's all. So, will you do it?"

Alicia pauses. "Okay. Wait till I record the numbers."

"You've got a tape recorder in your phone?"

"No. My dad got me this tiny dictation thingy last

year. It's like a notepad. I can record stuff and then play it back a couple times till it's memorized. My memory's gotten pretty good."

"Cool."

Then I tell her the information about the blanket, and the number at Sears, and she says she'll call me back.

Twenty minutes later, I've got my mouth full of English muffin and the cell phone rings. "Hi. What's the news?"

"No news. These people aren't giving anything away."

"What happened?"

"I told the guy who answered in the legal office that I was doing a product liability inquiry about blanket model number so-and-so, and three seconds later this lady named Amber Carson picks up. Real serious. So I tell her I'm investigating a complaint from a family in Chicago about this blanket, and right away she just shuts down, tells me nothing. I asked her how many complaints they've had. She says, 'I'm not at liberty to share that information.' She says, 'Send me a letter,' and that was it. End of conversation." After a pause Alicia adds, "I'm sure they have a list of people who've returned those blankets, but there's no way they're giving out any names."

"And you think the records are in the legal department somewhere?"

"Sure. In their computer system. They've probably got a whole team working on bad products and recalls and claims. But think about it: If you were them, would you hand that information over just because someone asks?"

"No," I say, "but who said anything about asking? If they've got it, then we go and take it."

Alicia laughs. "You're kidding, right?"

"Am I?" There's a hard edge to my voice, and a plan forms as I talk. "You're the one who said I shouldn't just sit around for five days and do nothing, remember? So are you ready for a little field trip?"

Alicia is stunned. "What? . . . Go out there and try to *steal* the information? And what do you mean, am *I* ready? What do I have to do with any of this?"

I'm the Greek warrior again, more like a general now, planning my campaign, getting my troops ready for battle. "Simple. I can get inside the building, find the right office, get the information, and then print out a list or make a disk or something, but I can't carry floating paper or plastic around, at least not for very long. If I was a hacker and had a week to try to invade their computer system, I would. But I don't know how to do that, and I don't have a week. So I need someone to help. My parents and your parents are the only other candidates. Since I don't think they'd get behind the idea of stealing corporate secrets, that leaves you."

"But . . . you could just do like when you went to the hospital to visit your mom."

"No way. Too warm today. If it's sixty-five degrees and you wear gloves and a stocking hat and sunglasses and a scarf around your face, you look like a bank robber. And then once I got there looking very suspicious,

I'd have to have a place to take off my clothes and hide them, and then come back and get them—it's too complicated. I need your help, Alicia. You be my body, and I'll be your eyes. Help me hail a cab, and talk to the driver and pay the fare, wait for me to come back and hand off the stuff, then we take a cab home again."

Silence. Then she says, "What if you don't come back? Like if something happens to you?" I like the way she says that, the tone of her voice. But I keep being the warrior.

"Nothing's going to happen. I'm the secret weapon, remember? And even if something did happen, like if it took too long and I didn't come back to you on time— say, after an hour—then you find someone to help you get a cab, you tell the guy your address, and you come home. And I'd take care of myself. But I'm sure it'll be all right. So, what do you think? Can you get out, like, tell your mom you're going to the library early or something?"

"Yeah . . . I think I can get out. . . . Bobby, are you sure this is worth doing?"

"Sure? How could I be sure? Of course I'm not sure. But it beats doing nothing, right?"

". . . I guess so. . . . What about cab money?"

"All set. I've got enough cash, my own money, birthdays and stuff. And if we run out, I can just walk into a restaurant or some store, and I'll help myself to the register . . . or maybe I'll try a little pickpocketing."

No response.

"I'm joking, Alicia, I'm joking."

"Not funny, Bobby." No smile in the voice.

"C'mon, Alicia, lighten up. This'll be an adventure. Listen, you get all set, and be sure to bring your backpack, and I'll meet you at the corner of Fifty-seventh and Ellis in about twenty minutes, okay? . . . And if you're not there, then I'll come back home and call to see what's happened. Okay?"

". . . Okay."

"Good. See you in twenty minutes." Then I push the end button on the phone before she has a chance to think some more. Because if she did that, really thought about it, she'd probably say "No way!" And maybe she'd be right.

So I run up to my room, pull off my clothes, and roll up a handful of twenty-dollar bills.

On my way through the kitchen, I stop and write a short note:

> Mom—gone to Alicia's. I'll call you later.
> Bobby

And that's true. I probably will end up at Alicia's house. Just not right away.

And then I'm down the kitchen steps and out the side door. I'm off to commit my first real crime.

chapter 20

DESTINATIONS

A half hour later I'm shivering, standing at the corner of Fifty-seventh and Ellis. My hand is cramping up from holding the roll of money so tightly. I wait till the coast is clear and tuck the cash between my left arm and my rib cage, hidden by a layer of nonreflective flesh.

Alicia is late. I look at the bank clock and decide to give her until 11:22. Then I see her tapping toward me, and I start trotting the half block to meet her. It's too crowded, so I can't call out "Hey, Alicia!" or something.

I get close, and I'm about to say a quiet "Hi," but there's something about the look on Alicia's face that stops me. I look behind her and I see the problem. The blind girl has a shadow. It's her mom. Mrs. Van Dorn is about thirty feet back, holding a book open in one hand and glancing down at it every few steps so she won't look odd for walking so slowly.

Falling in step alongside Alicia, I whisper, "Don't stop, and don't look toward my voice—your mom is behind you."

Without breaking stride or turning her head, Alicia hisses, "I know! She can always tell when I'm lying, and it makes me crazy! And she's so stupid that she thinks I can't tell when she's following me! Our front door makes this squeaking groan, and I can hear it half a block away."

"So, what are you gonna to do?"

"Go to the library like I told her. And once I'm there, she'll get bored and leave."

We get to the library and Alicia goes in and up the elevator, and her mother just sits down on a bench out front, reading her book and glancing up at the doorway now and then.

The look on Mrs. Van Dorn's face makes me feel sorry for her. She seems so sad and alone. She's wearing the same look I keep seeing on Mom's face. I'll walk quietly into the den or the kitchen, and Mom will be in the middle of something, but stopped, not paying attention to the computer or the book she's reading, and she'll have that same kind of sad, distant look in her eyes. And I always have the feeling that she's thinking about me. I think Alicia's mom must do a lot of worrying too.

Ten minutes go by, and then Mrs. Van Dorn gets up, heaves a big sigh, puts her book under her arm, and starts walking slowly back toward her house. She can go be sad and lonely at home.

When I'm sure she's really gone, I go up to the third floor of the library, find Alicia, and in five minutes we're looking for a cab to take us to the Sears corporate headquarters in Hoffman Estates.

The first two cabs refuse the fare, and I don't blame them. It's about a forty-mile trip. The third cabby looks at Alicia and says, "For you, fifty-five dollars—one-way.

Okay?" I whisper, "Okay," Alicia nods to the driver, and we get inside. When we're settled, I take her right hand and press my money into her palm.

Our driver heads straight for Lake Shore Drive north. There's a thick metal-and-Plexiglas divider between the front and back seat, plus, the driver's listening to some tinny music. Greek, I think. So Alicia and I talk softly about the plan. Which is pretty basic: I go snoop, she waits. I come back, we leave.

"But where should I wait? I can't just hang around in some lobby for an hour."

"Of course you can. Lobbies are made for loitering."

"Great. I just love to loiter."

So I say, "Fine. Here's a better idea. When we get there, you can ask somebody where you go to get a job application."

Alicia wrinkles her nose. "A job application? Me?"

"Sure. Companies love it when . . . um . . . people like you apply for jobs."

The eyebrows go up. "People like *me*?" she says. "You mean people with disabilities, right? Go ahead and say what you mean, Bobby. I know I've got a disability, okay? I'm not a baby. Just say it—disability!"

The driver is craning his neck, looking at Alicia in his mirror, uneasy about this angry outburst from his lone passenger.

I whisper, "Shh, the driver. Okay, okay: people who have disabilities. They'll be happy to interview you because they actually have to prove that they try to hire everyone. It's a federal law or something."

Alicia hisses, "It's called the Americans with Disabilities Act, Mr. Smartguy, and I know all about it, okay?"

"Fine." And I sit back and look out the window past the lakeside park to the choppy waters of Lake Michigan. A mile or so out to sea, a huge tanker is steaming north. I wish I were on it.

Once we're on the Kennedy Expressway, we start talking again and work out the rest of the plan. Nothing much to it.

And then I look out the window and start counting the planes circling O'Hare Airport. I spot seven without even trying.

Then I start watching Alicia's face. And it's amazing to me, because I can look at everything—the whole overpopulated, overtraveled, overtrucked, overpaved, overbillboarded, full-color, three-dimensional world zipping by at seventy miles an hour—and I can get bored. And Alicia's got nothing but her own thoughts and whatever she sees inside her head, and she's not bored at all. She's soaking up the trip. Completely alert. I watch, and she has a slight response to every little hum and thump of the tires, the jangling radio music, the flutter and rush of air in the window, the static and garbled bursts from the driver's two-way, the rumble of a big Kenworth tractor, the whine of a jet on approach, an ambulance screaming past on the eastbound side. A constant flow, bright, fresh pictures with every second. As we sway and bounce and change lanes and brake and accelerate and feel our way along the highway, her nostrils flare like a wild pony sniffing the wind, and I know Alicia's also processing the smells—the exhaust and kerosene, the accumulated scent of a thousand cab passengers, that half-eaten tin of salad on the seat by the driver—an ocean of airborne information to sift and sort.

And watching her, I'm not bored.

Still, it's a long ride. When we finally arrive, I'm not prepared for the scale of things. The concrete and glass buildings are huge, not tall, but wide and deep and far apart. The place looks more like a college campus than the home of a retail giant. It's like they took the whole huge, black Sears Tower, broke it up into short chunks, painted it with friendlier suburban colors, and then spread it out over two hundred acres of farmland. Bike paths, a fake pond or two, a basketball court, a huge day-care facility. Very pleasant. Unless you don't know where you're going.

The young woman at the reception desk inside the foyer of the main building looks at Alicia, takes in the whole picture, and then says, "Miss? May I help you find someone?"

Alicia goes to work. She faces the woman's voice, smiles, and says, "Yes. I'd like to speak with someone in the employment office. I don't have an appointment. I'm just looking for some information . . . about hiring practices for persons with disabilities."

"Of course. May I have your name?"

"Alicia Van Dorn."

"Please wait just a moment, Miss Van Dorn."

While the lady punches out numbers on her phone, I

scan the Sears Merchandise Group map and directory on the wall behind the desk. And I find what I need. Legal services is in a building about a quarter mile away.

I make a mental note of where the employment offices are, and now I can leave. That's what Alicia and I planned. She's going to do her thing, and I'm going to do mine. When I'm done, I find her. It was 11:45 when we got out of the cab. The deal is that if I don't find her by 1:15, she has someone call her a cab, and she goes back to the library in Hyde Park.

But I don't leave. I wait. And I can't talk, but I tap lightly on Alicia's cane, and she stiffens, then smiles slightly, and motions with her head and eyebrows, urging me to get going. But I wait anyway.

About two minutes pass, and a young man wearing chinos and a blue dress shirt with a loud tie comes out of a corridor and walks right over to Alicia. "Miss Van Dorn?"

Alicia turns and smiles. "Yes?"

"Hi. I'm John Freeman. I'm with personnel, and I'd be happy to try to answer your questions. Let's head this way. Would you like to take my arm?" He turns and offers his left arm, elbow crooked just right. He's helped blind people before. And he looks like a nice enough guy.

Alicia says, "Thanks," lifts the end of her cane off the floor, and takes hold of his elbow. And they're off.

And now I've got one hour and ten minutes to find the names of some unhappy customers.

chapter 21

FINDINGS

News flash: Invisible people make excellent spies and thieves.

Finding exactly what I want at the legal department is ridiculously easy.

Access through the security doors? A snap: I wait for a slow moving person of considerable size and slide through the doorway right behind his behind.

Finding the right information? A cinch: I've got a name to work with. Amber Carson is the woman who stonewalled Alicia on the phone about two and half hours ago. I find her office on the fourth floor, which is the only hard part, and then I wait patiently in an empty cubicle until she goes to lunch at 12:25.

Ms. Carson apparently trusts all her coworkers, because she doesn't log off of her computer. Which is good because it saves me the trouble of finding Alicia and telling her that this is going to take a lot longer—which it would have, because I'd have had to wait until Amber Carson got back from lunch, then I'd have had to look over her shoulder to learn her password, and then wait for her to leave her office again so I could use her computer.

I don't know if I could ever be a good lawyer. Lawyers are organized. The folks at Sears keep their files in such good order that I bet I could start from nothing and find whatever I needed in fifteen minutes or less. But I don't even have to do an actual search. That's because I've got inside information. I happen to know that Amber Carson accessed the very file I'm looking for earlier today when Alicia called her. So all I have to do is use the "Recent Documents" utility on her computer: point, click, and there it is. Which is kind of a shame. I went to a lot of trouble to memorize the model number of the blanket—all ten characters—and now I don't even need to use it.

The database notes show the entire history of my doomed electric blanket. Turns out 9,308 blankets were sold before it was discovered that some percentage of the controller units had been manufactured with faulty resistors. As of today, 379 consumers have complained, and of those, 163 have accepted a new blanket. When the problem was first noticed, the legal counsel had advised that there should be no product recall, but rather, Customer Service should go with a "replace as requested" plan. Only one customer had complained that he believed the blanket made his heart pacemaker malfunction, but there was no injury and no lawsuit. Still, to be on the safe side, the legal staff set the policy that any complaining customer with a pacemaker should be advised to discontinue use of the blanket and return it immediately for refund, credit, or exchange.

I'm glad I know enough about computers, because all I really want from the file is the list of 379 people who complained about the blanket. And with a couple simple sort functions, I've got their names and addresses and phone numbers isolated in a list. Printing out the list would make a big stack of paper—unless you know how to format, which I do. And it turns out that Amber Carson is an important enough person in the Sears legal department to have her own little laser printer on a worktable by a window that looks out over the rolling lawn. So I put the whole list into seven-point type, single-space it, format it into six columns, and print it out. I end up with just three pages—very small type, but readable.

I fold the stack of pages inward from top to bottom three times, and then fold the result in half lengthwise twice more. What I end up with is a wad of paper about an inch wide and two inches long, the perfect size to stick up into my left armpit—gross and uncomfortable, but effective. As long as I keep my left arm clamped against my side, the paper is completely hidden.

By 12:47, I'm on my way to hunt for Alicia. I could just go to the main entrance and wait for her, because that was our plan. But what's the fun of that? I'd rather track her down.

I glide through three different doors, then down one stairwell, along one corridor, through one last door, and then I'm outside.

It's a lot more springlike in Hoffman Estates than it was in Hyde Park. People are all over the place, eating lunch, resting, talking with friends. They look like creatures who have crawled out of burrows to soak up some sunlight. Except for the smokers. There's a little group of them outside almost every doorway, standing around, looking sort of defensive. They're not outside for the fresh air. I hold my breath when I go past so I don't have to smell the stuff.

The map at the reception area said the personnel offices are in a building that's close to the main entrance. Again I wait for someone to help me through the security doors. Once inside, I'm lost. I'm on the ground floor, and it's an area about the size of three football fields. There are partitions and corridors, nice offices around the perimeter, paintings and posters everywhere, bright and cheery, but it's still like a maze. This is an employees-only area, so there are no signs, no helpful maps or diagrams except for the occasional emergency evacuation poster.

So I just wander. My shoulder is aching and my arm is starting to go to sleep from the pressure of the clump of paper in my armpit. I'm almost ready to give up and head for our rendezvous spot.

Then I hear Alicia's laugh, complete with that little snort at the end. I follow the sound to a glass-walled conference room where she's sitting with a bottle of Snapple and a thick blue folder on the table in front of her. Alicia's smiling and nodding, moving her head to follow the voices of the people at the table. She looks like she could have just graduated from college. With honors. And three proposals of marriage.

Apparently the guy who picked her up from reception is the big joker, because as I approach, he says something I can't quite hear, and Alicia and the two other people in the room start cackling again. Also at the table

183

is a man who looks as old as my dad, but with a wrinkly face with a gray mustache and not much hair up top. He's wearing incredibly thick glasses. The fourth person is a woman who's maybe thirty, maybe younger. She's got short blond hair and big earrings, and she's wearing a soft gray pants-and-jacket outfit with a pink shirt. A nice enough face, a good smile, but squinting. Then I see this lady's like Alicia. She's got a white cane on the floor by her chair.

The meeting's just breaking up, and I'm outside looking in. I get too close to the glass, and my breath fogs it up, so I move back a little. I watch Alicia. She shakes hands, first with the older man and then the woman. The smiles and handclasps are so strong, so real and warm. And it's like this wave sweeps over me, and my eyes get blurry, and I swallow hard. Alicia takes the arm of the younger man, and I turn and walk away fast. I don't want her to know I saw any of this. I don't want her to feel like I've been spying on her. I know she came on this trip to help me out. But this meeting she just had? These people she's met and talked to and laughed with? This is something she's done on her own. It's part of her life, not mine. It's got nothing to do with me.

I'm in the reception area when Alicia and her guide appear, and I keep well away. Another warm handshake, then he's gone, and the woman at the desk says, "Alicia, I noticed you arrived by cab earlier. Would you like me to call one for you?"

Alicia hesitates, so I hurry over and gently tap on her cane. She's startled, but doesn't show it, and then says to the lady, "Yes, that'd be great. And be sure the driver knows this is for a ride to Hyde Park in Chicago. Some drivers don't want to go that far. And thank you."

"Certainly. We get good service from the local cab company. They'll take you wherever you need to go. There's a bench to the left outside the front entrance if you'd like to wait outdoors. Otherwise, I can show you to a seat inside the doorway."

Alicia smiles again, says, "Thanks," and heads for the doorway.

Thinking I'll be helpful, I take hold of her cane out in front of her hand. She stops and shakes her head sharply. I pull my hand away, and then follow her outside. I wait until she's found the bench and sits down.

No one's near, so I say, "I got in, and I printed out a long list of names. Can I put it in your backpack?"

Alicia nods, swings the pack off her back, and unzips the main compartment, holding it open. There in the bag I can see the thick blue folder that she had in the conference room. I glance around, take the list from under my arm, and drop it in. Alicia feels it hit the backpack, so she pulls the zipper closed, swings the bag behind her, and loops the straps back over her shoulders. She whispers, "So, you got something?"

And I whisper back, "Yeah."

The cab that arrives has no divider between the front and back seat, so I can't talk to Alicia. There's nothing to do but settle back in the seat and look out the window.

The outer highways aren't too crowded, but when we

get closer to O'Hare, everything bogs down. The cab is crawling through afternoon traffic, I'm three feet away from two other people, and I can't talk to either of them. I've never felt this alone. And the worst part is that Alicia seems perfectly content not to talk. She seems glad that she doesn't even have to try.

The driver looks up into his mirror and says, "My sister? She works at Sears out in Rockford. Good company, y'know? Good benefits."

Alicia nods and smiles, then turns her face toward the window. The cabby makes a few other attempts to get a conversation going, but Alicia just nods or murmurs a little, so the guy gives up and punches up a country station on the radio.

It's a slow ride home. It's almost three, and right on schedule, the cab arrives at my house. I've got the list of names stuffed back under my arm. The driver puts the car into park and says, "That'll be fifty-eight dollars, miss."

Alicia pushes her door open and I scramble out. Then I lean back inside and I whisper, "Call you later. And thanks."

Alicia nods slightly to me, then faces the cabby and says, "I'm sorry—I just remembered an errand I have to run. Could you drop me at the big library on Fifty-sixth Street between University and Ellis?" Because that was our plan.

The driver shrugs and puts the car back in gear. "It's your money."

Alicia closes her door, and the cab pulls away. I watch her go.

There's a gust of wind from the east, and I shiver. I turn to go inside.

And I feel like something has ended. Or maybe begun. Or maybe both.

chapter 22

CALLS FIFTY-NINE
AND SIXTY

After I'm home, and after I get Mom off my case for being gone so long, and after I get my door locked and put on some clothes, I unfold the list and flatten it out. I stare at the names and I think about how I got them, and I'm not proud of myself for being a sneak thief. But it had to be done. Because something had to be done. Can't just sit around and do nothing.

And I think about Alicia. I feel like I should call to make sure she got home okay. But she'd probably just get all hissy about how she can take care of herself. So I root around in my desk until I find a clipboard and put the list on it. Then I pull the cell phone loose from the charger wire, flop down on my bed, and go to work.

My first fifty-eight phone calls to the people on the blanket list break down like this:

- thirteen phone service messages that say stuff like, "This number is no longer in service";
- eight answering machines that I don't leave messages on;
- six husbands who don't know their wives had done any such thing as exchange an electric blanket, and who couldn't care less;

- five wives who don't know their husbands had exchanged an electric blanket, and who also couldn't care less;
- six lonely old people who remember something about a bad electric blanket, but who really just want to talk to me about their grandchildren, or *Wheel of Fortune*, or the weather, or the cost of heating oil, or anything at all;
- eight people who hang up because they think I'm trying to sell something;
- six kids who don't know when Mom or Dad will be home, or who say Mom or Dad can't or doesn't want to come to the phone, and could I call back later;
- and six people—two men and four women— who are actually pleasant and cooperative, but had no strange blanket events to tell me about.

Fifty-eight phone calls and not one hint about anything unusual that might have happened because an electric blanket had stopped working properly.

Mom has gotten over being mad about me going out today without telling her anything. Dad has come home from the lab for dinner, but he doesn't smile about anything. I can tell he's still churning the data. And for two and a half hours before dinner and two and a half hours after dinner, I'm in my room going through the names from my crumpled stolen list. I'm lying on my bed, microwaves burning up my brain, running up a killer phone bill.

So it's about quarter of ten, and I make the fifty-ninth call. I know it's kind of late, but I skip ahead two names to a person who lives in Denver, because it's an hour earlier there.

"Mr. Borden?"

"Yes?"

"Sorry to bother you at home, but I'm doing a survey about your experience with a Sears electric blanket."

"A blanket?"

"Yes, from Sears. Do you recall exchanging the blanket?"

"Yeah, we had a pink one. It was prob'ly my wife did it. But it wasn't really our blanket. It was just . . . left here."

"Left there? You mean at your home?"

The man doesn't answer at once. His voice is strained. "My daughter. Sheila. That was her blanket."

"May I please talk with her, then?"

"No, she's . . . she's gone now."

I hear the catch in his voice. And that certain way he uses the word "gone."

I don't know what to say. "Oh. I . . . I'm so sorry, Mr. Borden. I hope you don't mind me asking, but this is pretty important. Do you think your daughter's death had anything to do with the electric blanket?"

"Death?" he says. There's anger in his voice. "She's not dead. That's the hell of it. She's just . . . gone. Over three years now."

I feel the hair on my arms stand up—invisible goose

bumps. "Gone, you mean like . . . how? Like run away from home? Something like that?"

The man blows his nose, clears his throat. "Don't really know. She dropped out of college, moved back home, gets a job. Then she takes up with some of her old friends, starts staying out late. Came home drunk most nights. Sleeps next day till noon, gets up, goes to her job at the restaurant, and on like that for about two months. Then one night she comes in late, goes to bed, and the next morning . . . gone."

". . . And you haven't heard from her since?"

"Only once. She called, asked could we send her two thousand dollars—two thousand *more* than the four she already stole when she left. Send it Western Union, she says, to this grocery store in Florida. So I did it. Probably stupid, but if you have kids, you know why I had to do it. That's about two years ago. Since then, nothing—'cept a note last Christmas. And it's not like it was even a card or something nice for her mother. Just one of those computer messages."

My heart almost stops. "You mean an e-mail?"

"I guess so. It's just plain letters on a piece of typing paper. Sent it to Mrs. Harlan's house next door, then her boy made a copy on his computer and brought it over to us."

"Mr. Borden, it's really important that I talk to your daughter. Do you still have that message your neighbor brought to you?"

"You kiddin'? My wife keeps everything—pictures,

191

bits of hair, baby shoes, first tooth, report cards—everything. Tore her up when Sheila left."

"Could you find that paper for me?"

"You mean right now?"

"Please . . . if it's not too much trouble. It might be a big help."

"Hang on. I've got to walk upstairs."

I'm on my feet now, pacing. I go over to my desk and open up a little notebook. My hands are so sweaty, it's hard to hold the ballpoint. He's taking a long time.

There's a click on the line as Mr. Borden picks up another extension.

"You still there?"

"Yes, sir."

"Okay. Here's what it says: 'Dear Mom and Dad, I just wanted to say Merry Christmas. I know I left so suddenly, but I think it was the best thing for all of us. Sorry if it hurt you. I think about you a lot, and I hope I can come home to see you again. Love, Sheila.' "

I don't want to hear all this, but once he's started, I can't interrupt. His voice is thick at the end, and when he stops, I say, "Mr. Borden, at the top of the page, is there something that has the 'at' symbol in it—a little 'a' inside a circle? It might even say 'From,' and then have a bunch of letters or numbers?"

I'm holding my breath. "Yeah, up at the top. It says 'From,' and then there's something like that."

"Can you please spell it out for me, just exactly the way it's written?"

"It's not written, it's all typed."

"That's what I mean. Just the way it's typed."

"It says 'e-i-l-a-s-h,' then that 'at' doohickey, then it says 'g-l-o-w-z' and then a period, and then 'n-e-t'—'net.' And that's all of it."

"Mr. Borden, thanks so much for your help. I really appreciate it."

"Well, you're welcome. And I hope you can fix this blanket problem of yours."

"Thanks. Me too."

I push the button to end the call, and I see the phone wobbling. That's because my hands are shaking. Maybe this is nothing, just a coincidence. But if there's anything at all to find out, I will. Because now I have Sheila Borden's e-mail address: eilash@glowz.net. Her dad probably never even noticed that "eilash" is just "Sheila" mixed around a little. That's probably the only e-mail he ever got in his life.

Dad and Mom are both in the study, sitting in the big armchairs on either side of the tall reading lamp. Dad is dozing, a clipboard with notes and diagrams lying in his lap. Mom looks up from her book and smiles when my clothes walk in. I sit down at the computer, and she frowns.

"It's almost bedtime, Bobby."

"I just have to use the Net a few minutes."

She goes back to her book, and when the computer is ready, I open up a search engine. I find the people search features, and jump around until I see what I need. It's a reverse-hunt engine: You put in an e-mail address, and unless the person you are looking for has been a freak about online privacy, that e-mail address leads you right to the rest of their data.

So I scroll to the right box, and I key in "eilash@ glowz.net."

I've got her: Sheila Borden lives in Miami, and I've got her street address and her phone number!

When I shout, Dad sits up straight and his clipboard clatters to the floor. Mom stares over her book at me.

"What?"

"Oh, sorry. Nothing. Just found a cool website, that's all." Because I don't want to jinx this. It's probably nothing, and besides, I don't want to get stuck trying to explain about my field trip to Sears for the rest of the night.

"Well, it's your bedtime. And you too, David. You've been sitting here snoring, so don't tell me you've got work to do. Up now, both of you."

I grab the printout, say "Good night," and I'm back up to my room, two steps at a time. I shut my door and grab the phone off my bed, and then I stand still. Part of me says, "Go back down there and talk to the folks, tell them what you're thinking here, ask for some advice." But I don't want to. This is my deal this time, not theirs. Part of me says, "Call this Sheila right now and see what she has to say." But I don't want to do that either. And part of me says, "Call Alicia."

That's the part of me I agree with. So I punch in her number.

"Hello?"

"Oh—hi, Mrs. Van Dorn. This is Bobby. I'm really sorry to be calling so late. Could I talk to Alicia?"

Long pause. "Bobby, did you go somewhere with Alicia this afternoon?"

My head kicks up into overdrive. In two seconds I think: *If she's asking me this, does it mean she already knows, and this is a test to see if I'm a liar? Or is she just suspicious—fishing for info?*

I say, "I did see her at the library, if that's what you mean." Because that's true, and now it's her turn to give me another clue about where this is coming from. I'm a pro at this game.

I can hear the worry in her voice. "She was out almost four hours this afternoon, and she won't talk to me about it. Do you know anything else?"

Aha. The mom doesn't know. She's fishing. This next part has to be just right, or I'm blacklisted by the mother and hated by the daughter. The first would be an inconvenience; the second would be a tragedy.

So I say, "If you don't mind, Mrs. Van Dorn, I don't think it's my place to get between one of my friends and her parents." Nice—no, better than nice—brilliant. And it hits me: Three weeks ago I couldn't have even *thought* that, much less said it to somebody like Alicia's mom.

Another pause, plus a mom-sigh. "Yes, I suppose you're right, Bobby. I'll call Alicia."

And while I wait, I'm thinking maybe I should become a family counselor, or maybe a hostage negotiator.

"Bobby?"

"Hi, Alicia."

"Just a minute." Then away from the phone she yells, "Mother? Hang UP!"

And I hear the other phone click off.

"She always tries to eavesdrop. So, did my mom say anything to you?"

"She asked me if I went somewhere with you today."

"And you said . . ."

"That I did see you at the library. And then she said you wouldn't tell her where you were for four hours, and did I have any information, and then I said I didn't think I should get between a friend and her parents."

"You said *that*?!"

"I did. And she said, 'Yes, I suppose you're right.' You may applaud now, or throw flowers if you wish."

"I'm impressed."

"I knew you would be. That's why I told you."

"Okay, smart guy. So what did you do when you got home?"

"You mean after I dealt with *my* mother?"

"Of course."

"I made a jillion phone calls—fifty-eight duds, and then I hit the jackpot . . . maybe. Or maybe it's just another dead end. The father of a girl who went to bed one night, and in the morning, she's all gone."

"Like *gone* gone?"

"Don't know. She hasn't been home in about three years, but she sent an e-mail to her folks last Christmas, and I got her e-mail address, and then I looked up her address and phone."

"You called her?"

"I . . . I wanted to talk to you first."

"Oh." And then, "How come?"

"To see what you think I should say to her."

"How should I know?"

"I mean, I can't just call up and say, 'I know you had this defective pink blanket, and that you left home very suddenly—so tell me, Sheila, are you invisible?' I can't say something like that, or she'll just hang up. And besides, it's pretty late."

Alicia's quiet for about ten seconds. "Bobby?"

"What?"

Another pause, and then it's her quiet voice. "You're very smart. You know exactly how to talk to this woman. I know that. So why did you call me?"

For the second time during this phone call, I've got to get something just right, first try. "Because this afternoon . . . because it felt like we rode out there to Sears together, and . . . and then we came home alone. And I didn't like it."

Silence. And I'm thinking I've said too much or maybe too little or maybe just the completely wrong thing because I'm an idiot.

But she says, "That's my fault—but don't think it's because I didn't want to be with you or help you . . . or that I don't like you, because I do like you. It's . . . it's because I talked with those people about being blind and working . . . like really working in a real job at a big company and everything. I mean, some lady at the Lighthouse talked to me about all the jobs there are for

197

blind people, but that was like a year ago, and I didn't believe it had anything to do with me. But today, it was different. And it was so new. To think about myself that way. And it was scary, and . . . and it made feel alone. It made me feel alone."

"Oh."

She opens up her heart to me, and what do I say? I say "Oh." And I'm so mad at myself. Because I could have said, "But you're not alone, Alicia. I'm here. I'll always be here." And then the lights would dim, and the violins would start playing, and I take her face between my hands . . . oh, jeez. I am in big trouble.

Right away I say, "But it's good, what happened to you. Maybe you meeting those people was what today was really about, you know what I mean? Because this Sheila woman, and all the other two hundred and some people on my list? Maybe all that is nothing, like . . . nothing. But what happened for you today, that was real, right? So that's good."

"Yeah. It was good. I think that's true."

Then things feel awkward, and for a second I'm afraid I might have said that stuff I was thinking right out loud, or else maybe Alicia used her real eyes, and she saw what I was feeling. Right through the telephone. Her real eyes.

I say, "So, listen. I'll call this lady tomorrow, and then let you know what happens, okay?"

"Okay."

"And thanks, Alicia."

"For what?"

"For today, I guess. For everything."

"Everything?"

"Yeah."

"You're welcome. And thank you too, Bobby."

"For what?"

"Same thing."

"Bye."

"Good night."

As I get ready for bed, and then turn off the lights and pull up the feather quilt, I'm not thinking about my electric blanket and how much I miss it. I'm not thinking about Sheila Borden, or about her dad—call number fifty-nine.

I'm thinking about call number sixty, my call to Alicia.

chapter 23

LONG-LOST SISTER

I half wake up, wrestling with a dream. This guy named Hoffman has kidnapped Alicia and locked her away in a tower, and I'm going nuts looking for a way inside. Then I discover a secret panel that looks like thick pink glass, but it's just a hologram, and I walk right through it. Inside, Alicia is chained to a table, and these electrodes are hooked to her temples, and she's straining at her chains, and beams of sharp green light are shooting out of her eyes and burning holes in the ceiling. Hoffman is wearing a caveman suit made out of old brown pants tied on with neckties, and he's got his hands on the power dials, and behind him there are two jail cells with Mom in one and Dad in the other.

I sit up in bed and force myself to wake up. The clock on my dresser says 9:20. And I know it's Wednesday, and I'm in my house in Hyde Park. And I'm glad all that was a dream. Not that reality is a whole lot better. Or less random. And I don't like that image of Mom and Dad behind bars. I have to shake off a feeling of dread. Because if you let it, the fear just keeps coming.

I do my best thinking in the shower. It's so odd to see the tiny streams of water bounce around, see the shapes of my hands and arms and legs. Warm water runs down my back, and I plan out my talk with Sheila Borden.

Because that's the big event for today. Maybe the biggest event in my life. And maybe hers too.

I turn off the water and drip dry a little, slide back the curtain, and step out of the tub. And there's no towel. I open the door, and I'm about to yell and see if Mom is still home. But I hold the yell just in time. Because I hear Mom talking down in the entry hall. And I know the voice that answers her. It's Ms. Pagett. I creep to the banister at the top of the stairwell. I can't see either of them, but the acoustics are great.

"The problem? The problem is that I've now heard from the Florida authorities, Mrs. Phillips. They have called and visited the home of Mrs. Ethel Leighton and have gotten no response, day or night. Seems your aunt Ethel has vanished. So we'd like you to tell us where she and your son might be."

Mom laughs lightheartedly and says, "Well, that's Aunt Ethel for you. She's a little flighty sometimes. When I talked with her Monday afternoon, she said Bobby was feeling so much better. She said they might do some day trips, maybe even go up to Orlando."

"But surely, Mrs. Phillips, you must know where your own son is. You don't seem worried at all."

"Why should I be worried? Aunt Ethel is my father's sister, and I have known her all my life—and I've known Bobby all of his life. They are two very stable people, and I'm sure they're just fine, and when they get a chance, they'll check in. And I am so sorry that this is proving difficult for you and your friends in Florida."

Ms. Pagett takes her time answering. "Mrs. Phillips, this isn't difficult. Difficult is when a child is declared to be formally missing under suspicious circumstances. Because at that point, the full resources of the state of Illinois jump into action—and possibly the FBI as well. When that happens, these things often get into the newspapers. It can affect lives and careers. It can get quite messy, and . . . difficult."

"That sounds a lot like a threat, Miss Badger."

"My name is Ms. Pagett, and it's not a threat. It's a promise."

Mom pauses. "Do they teach the people in your agency anything about the United States Constitution? One of the best ideas in the Constitution is that little part about how a citizen shall be presumed innocent until proven guilty. *Proven.* Tell me, did you happen to bring along another search warrant this morning?"

"No."

"Fine. Then you have a nice day, Miss Pagett."

And the front door slams shut.

It can't be a good idea, treating the woman like that. I'm not sure I like having Mom act like some tough guy from a Clint Eastwood movie. But as with almost everything else these days, it's out of my hands. So I get on with the business of finding a towel.

As I grab a quick breakfast, Mom is cleaning up in the kitchen. She doesn't say anything about Ms. Pagett, and I don't ask. But I can tell she's on edge. I'm glad she has a ten o'clock class. It'll get her mind off the long arm of the law, and it'll also get her out of my way.

Ten minutes later, Mom's gone, and I'm at the desk in my room. I have some notes on a pad of paper. I know what I'll say if I get an answering machine, what I'll say if Sheila picks up herself, what I'll say if it's a kid or a boyfriend or someone. And I think I know how I can get her to tell me if she knows anything useful.

And as I punch in her phone number, I'm being careful. For myself, I mean. I'm being careful not to get my hopes up. I'm just going to ask this lady a few questions. If her answers help, fine. If they don't, then I go back to the big list and call another hundred, another two hundred people—whatever it takes to see whatever there is to see. Which might just be nothing. Or everything.

"Yes?" And then a throaty cough. A woman's voice, sleepy. The voice of someone who smokes cigarettes.

"Sheila Borden?"

"Yes, that's right." Awake now, on guard.

"I'm calling because I think you might be able to—"

"Are you one of those kids from Students Against Drunk Driving? Because I already said no to you people two days ago."

"No, it's nothing like that. I'm calling because of something else. I'm calling because I talked with your father last night. And—"

"You talked with my father? About me?" Now there's an edge in her voice—fear, maybe a little anger.

"No, not really about you, not specifically." And this is the scary part of my plan. Because I've decided to just tell the truth. Because it takes truth to find truth, right?

That's what my dad says. And what's the risk? She has no idea who I am. I'm just this voice on the phone. So I say, "I called your dad because I woke up one morning about three and half weeks ago and I was . . . *gone.* Just like you."

Tick, tick, tick. Then she says, "What are you talking about? You got up one morning and you ran away from home?"

And I notice she's not hanging up on me. She's talking, thinking.

I say, "I didn't run away from home. From school, yes—but only kind of." I pause, because I want her to have time to think. "I was just . . . *gone.*"

She's angry now. "Is this some kind of a prank? I don't believe you talked to my father. Anybody could call anybody and say that. What's his address and phone number?"

I'm ready for that one. I read off the information.

"Okay, so you talked to my dad. So what? What's this got to do with me? How come you're calling?"

So I use my big question. "When I say that I woke up one morning and I was 'gone,' what do you think I mean by that?"

Just the slightest hesitation, then she says, "How should I know what you mean?"

"Just take a guess. That's all I'm asking. First guess?"

"Like I said . . . that you ran away from home."

"Nope. Guess again."

". . . You didn't know who you were—amnesia or something."

"That's closer. Guess again."

"Hey, you know what? Good-bye, that's what!"

And she slams her phone down so hard that I hear it bounce off onto the floor, hear her swearing and grabbing for it, and then a second slam, and the line goes dead. And I'm afraid I've lost her. Really afraid.

I punch redial. Two, three, five rings, and the answering machine picks up. It's her voice on the message, all bright and cheery and efficient: "This is Sheila at Eilash Technical. Leave a message, or send an e-mail from our website, Eilash dot com. That's E-I-L-A-S-H dot com. Bye."

Then there's the beep, and I'm rushing. I'm rushing to say everything, and I'm talking way too fast, and I'm probably saying too much, but I don't care. "Sheila? I didn't mean to get you mad or anything. I'm just trying to find something out. Because I . . . I really did wake up that morning, and I really was gone. Like I couldn't see myself. That's what I mean. And I'm trying to figure it out, I *have* to figure it out, I *have* to, and I just thought that if—"

She picks up the phone and I hear her answering machine click off. There's a deep tiredness in her voice, a weariness. "You can't just call someone up and say, 'I turned invisible one day,' can you?"

And I know. I don't believe it yet, but I know. I gulp, and I feel tears at the corners of my eyes. Because it's like I'm finding a lost sister or something . . . like a reunion with an army buddy, an old Greek warrior. "So . . . so it really did happen to you too?"

Almost a whisper. "Really." Then, "How did you find me?"

So I tell her, and she's blown away. "A *blanket*? That's so wild! A blanket? From Sears . . ." She pauses, then, "Oh, man . . . we could be talking about a *big* lawsuit here. *Sears,* for God's sake! *Big* money, do you realize that? Millions!"

She wants to talk. I can tell that. But I look at my notes, and I have to keep to my own program.

"So, can you remember the date that it happened to you?"

She laughs, and there's bitterness in it. "What do you think? Of course I can. January twelfth, three years ago. Hard to forget a day that totally scrambles your life, don't you think?"

And then she needs to talk, and I listen to her whole story. How she panicked that morning, how she started to tell her parents, but then stopped. She actually lived at home three days after it happened. She saw her parents crying about her. She lived in her own room, learned to sneak around, learned how to carry small stuff between her arms and her rib cage. She stole her dad's savings account information, went to the public library, used the Internet, and transferred four thousand dollars into the account she had used at college. Then she set up an account for herself at a bank in Miami and transferred the money there. She stole it because she didn't know what else to do. Which tells me a lot about her, and about me. Because the first thing I did when it happened was tell my parents. She didn't feel like she could do that.

I ask, "Why Florida?"

"Why do you think? Ever try walking around naked in Denver in the wintertime?"

And I see why she went south. She took a plane. Just rode the bus to Denver International, found a flight that wasn't too full, and walked on. Sat up in first class and stole food from people who were sleeping.

At a public access terminal in a Miami library, she found a cheap apartment and paid the deposit electronically.

"Didn't you have to sign papers or something? Like, in person?"

"Ever see a Muslim woman completely covered in a black veil? That's what I did. No one even blinked. I wear it when I go grocery shopping too. There's a pretty good sized Islamic community around here. The only bad part is when I'm at the supermarket, and another veiled woman comes over and starts yakking at me in Farsi or Urdu or something, and all I can do is nod and say 'Salaam.' But other than that, it works great."

For the past three years, she's been earning good money designing websites. She bought a fast computer that was delivered to her door, bought some good software, and learned how to use it.

"I had plenty of time, know what I mean? And the Internet? It's made for people like me—like us. You don't ever have to go outside if you don't want to. I find design jobs on the Net, I work at home, I upload my projects over the Net, and I get paid by direct money transfer into my accounts. Works great."

"What about . . . like, friends?"

She laughs, but there's a hollow sound to it. "You mean, like, a boyfriend? Not a chance. I didn't like men that much back when they could see me. And they didn't like me so much either. I used to miss hanging out with my girlfriends from back home, but I'm over it. I had a parrot for a while, but it died. So this is simpler. I do my own thing, and that's all there is to it."

"What about doctors and dentists, stuff like that?"

"The only thing I worry about is if I get really sick. I had the flu last winter for about two weeks, and I almost thought I'd have to go to the hospital. But I just took a bunch of aspirin and toughed it out."

"How about if things got serious?"

"I've thought about that. First, I'd find a very rich woman doctor, the richer the better. And I'd walk into her offices wearing my black outfit. When we're alone, I'd remind her that she's required to keep my condition a secret, and I'd make her sign a promise of complete medical confidentiality. Then I'd take off my veils. And if she ever broke her promise, I'd sue her right down to her panty hose."

This lady's definitely a Greek warrior, only she's probably tougher than the guys were.

"So, no other friends?"

"Two. Both women. People I can trust. But that's

enough. Never had all that many friends anyway. How about you?"

"Kind of the same. At first it was just my parents. Then I started talking to this blind girl."

"Interesting—I thought about that too. So, does she know?"

"Yeah, but she's been great about everything. And her parents too."

"So, how long has it been for you? Less than a month?"

"Uh-huh, but I think there might be a way to reverse it. At least that's what I'm working on. And now I found you. If we figure it out, you'll be the first to know."

"So you really think there's a way back?"

"I hope so."

"Well, let me know, okay?"

"Absolutely. I will."

"What's your name?"

"Bobby. Bobby Phillips."

"It's nice to talk to you, Bobby."

"Yeah. It's good to talk to you too."

I don't know what else to say, and I'm about to sign off.

Then she says, "Bobby, you have to promise me something, okay?"

"Sure—I mean, I guess so. What?"

"I don't want you to tell anybody about me. Nobody."

"It's kind of too late. I already told Alicia I was going to call you. She's the blind girl."

"But she doesn't know anything else about me, right?"

"Yeah."

"So keep it that way. Don't tell her. Tell her you couldn't reach me or something. Tell her I'm dead, tell her whatever you want to."

"I . . . I don't want to lie to her. She'll keep everything a secret if I ask her to."

"Easy for you to say. What if she decides she needs money two years from now and she rats me out to some sleazy supermarket tabloid? Then what? Then I'm screwed, that's what."

"Alicia's not like that. Remember, she knows about me too. I trust her."

"But maybe that's because you're young and don't know any better. Or maybe you're stupid or something."

I'm about to start shouting when she says, "Sorry. I don't mean to sound nasty about this, but I've had to move twice in the last three years because I thought I could trust some people. Things like that happen, and it makes you pretty paranoid. . . . Well, look, if you've got to tell this girl, then I can't stop you, but don't tell anybody else, and make her *promise* to keep it a secret, okay? It's important. Do you understand?"

"Yes."

"And you promise?"

"I promise. And I know Alicia will too."

"Good. So . . . good luck. I hope everything works out the way you want it to."

"Thanks. Me too. And I'll get back in touch if there's any news."

After we say good-bye, I flop onto my bed and look at the ceiling. I need to take stock of what I know.

Three years. She's been gone for three years. So this is not a temporary condition. That's one thing I know.

This condition did have a specific cause, and the blanket is part of it. I'm sure of that now.

But the blanket's not all of it. If it was just the blanket causing this, then more people would have been affected. Then again, maybe more were and I just haven't called them yet.

And I know that it happened to Sheila on January twelfth three years ago in Denver, Colorado, and it happened to me February twenty-third—both in the winter. Duh. Big coincidence. Winter is when you use an electric blanket.

But still, I've got two locations, two blankets, and two dates. Plus two invisible people.

And lying there on my bed, tracing the maze of cracks in the plaster on my ceiling, I face a fact: What I've actually got is only slightly more than nothing.

chapter 24

FIRST-CLASS WORK

Any physics nut will tell you that there's never nothing. I've been hearing this from Dad all my life. Now I get it. For example, split the atom and you get neutrons and electrons and protons. Keep splitting and you get neutrinos and quarks and muons and antiquarks and mesons—on and on and on, smaller and smaller and smaller. Less and less mass, more and more energy.

It all gets down to the little things. Like two blankets, two cities, two dates, and two people.

After I talk to Sheila, I don't see how the facts can add up to anything. But it's never just about the facts. Sherlock Holmes proves that, case after case. It's all about what you do with the facts, how you look at them.

When I do an instant message to Alicia on Wednesday afternoon, she starts right in asking me a million questions about Sheila—how did she react, what did she sound like, was she happy, does she have a boyfriend, is she excited about finding someone else like her—on and on. Instant messaging with Alicia takes forever. It's not the connection, because she's got one of those lines that's always connected. It's because the text-to-speech function on her end has to say everything out loud before she can type back an answer.

I finally have to shut her off because I need to just

think about what to do. But Alicia doesn't want me to think about it. She wants me to call my dad and tell him the news, and then have my dad call her dad so they can talk about it.

bobby7272: no can do. i promised Sheila i wouldn't tell anyone about her. except you. i told her i had to tell you.

aleeshaone: had to? why?

bobby7272: isn't that obvious?

aleeshaone: maybe. tell me anyway

bobby7272: i told her I wouldn't lie to you

aleeshaone: so touching. still, u have to tell your dad and my dad. they can help.

bobby7272: i'll think about it

aleeshaone: don't think. do. time's up. it's time to do.

bobby7272: don't b bossy

aleeshaone: DO! DO! DO!

bobby7272: gotta go

aleeshaone: coward

bobby7272: m not

aleeshaone: r2

bobby7272: m not. i don't want to break a promise.

aleeshaone: so just give the dads the info. don't give the source. but they have to have the info. and maybe more. u might have to call your girlfriend back and talk real nice to her. all kissy kissy.

bobby7272: ha ha so funny

aleeshaone: so call your dad, ok?

aleeshaone: OK???

aleeshaone: BOBBY YOU ANSWER ME!!!!!
bobby7272: ok ok ok. bossy!!
aleeshaone: flattery will get you nowhere
bobby7272: i'm already nowhere
aleeshaone: so true
bobby7272: bye.
aleeshaone: let me know----promise???
bobby7272: promise. bye---bossy.

I start to dial Dad's number three times, and three times I stop. I found this woman. Not him. It's my discovery. Not his. But after I wrestle with it for about five minutes, I know I'd be stupid not to tell him. And I'll still be the one who found her. That's not going to change.

When I reach Dad at his office and tell him, he almost goes nuts.

"What?! You're kidding! This is fantastic, Bobby! Hold on—I've got to shut my office door."

Then comes the hard part, because he wants to know everything, but I'm not telling. "Dad, I promised to protect this other person. So all I know right now is that it happened in Denver, Colorado, on the night of January twelfth three years ago, and the same kind of blanket was being used."

"And this person is about how old?"

"Does that matter?"

"Could, Bobby. Everything could matter. Like what

214

kind of a house it happened in, any other appliances in the room, the exact location of the house—everything could be very important."

"Well, all I can tell you right now is the date and the year and the place. If we need more, I could maybe call her back and—"

"Aha! So, it's a woman! See, that could be important! Because men and women have different chemical make-ups, different muscle densities. We need more data, Bobby. The more the better."

Dad's giving me the third degree, major interrogation, and it really ticks me off. For the past few years I've just been gritting my teeth and kicking my door and swearing under my breath at him about stuff like this. I know he's excited, and I know that the guy lives for data. But here I am, and I'm telling him I've made a promise, and he acts like that doesn't matter.

I'm about to shout something and slam down the phone. But instead, I get this calm feeling and I say, real quietlike, "Dad, this lady wants to stay out of all this, and I promised her I'd respect that. So I'm not telling anyone, not even you. When I make a promise, it has to be real."

I guess I must have sounded like the president or something, and it's so quiet for a second that I think maybe he fell off his chair.

Then he says, "Of course. You're right. Sorry, Bobby. We'll work with this, and see where it leads us. Quite right, son. Have to keep your word."

And it's like the whole world has shifted about ten

feet to the right. I'm not where I used to be, and I see it, and Dad sees it too, and he sees me seeing him see me.

Anyway, he says he's going to call Leo—that's Professor Van Dorn—and he'll talk to me tonight when he gets home.

Then he says, "I don't know how you located this woman, Bobby, but it's not a small thing. This is first-class work, son. First class."

It's the tone of his voice that gets me.

He doesn't say, "I'm proud of you." He doesn't use those words. But that's what I hear. My dad's proud of me.

chapter 25

BINGO!

Relational database analysis. I had never even heard those words until Dad comes home from the lab and starts making dinner on Wednesday. He's got my invisible hands busy chopping celery and carrots while he cuts up chunks of chicken for a big pot of soup, and he's gushing about his talk with Dr. Van Dorn. The professor says he was sure the blanket was part of the cause, and he's all excited because he says he can do tons of research just using those two dates and the two locations. And that's because of this relational database thing.

Condensing fifteen minutes of Dad talking as fast as he can into about four sentences, this kind of data-hunting is basically like using an Internet search engine, except it's more precise and it uses monster computer power—like Cray supercomputers, the real deal. So you load in your data, you give the search program some clues about what sort of results you'd like it to look for, and then you push a button. And it combs all these scientific articles and catalogs of events and phenomena and facts and theories, and if anything matches up anywhere in the scientific records in any language anywhere in the world, it finds it and spits it all back at you. Pretty cool. But you have to know how to program the thing, or else you get swamped with junk data. And who's one of the top people at doing this kind of search? Our pal Dr. Van Dorn.

And an hour and a half later, when we're just sitting down to eat homemade chicken noodle soup, the doc himself is pounding on our front door.

He walks right in, puts his old briefcase on the dining room table, yanks it open, and pulls out a stack of wide greenbar computer paper. His eyes are wild, and he's talking so fast that little bits of spit are flying around. "This has got to be what we're looking for! I ran the search four different ways, four different sets of parameters, and the same data from the ACE spacecraft project kept showing up. Ready? Solar wind! January twelfth and February twenty-third, three years apart, and on both dates the upper latitudes of the U.S. from the Rockies to the Great Lakes were strafed by a major burst of accelerated solar particles and radiation—the kind that knock out power grids and send the big jets diving for lower altitudes! Not true solar maxima or anything, but the bombardment on both dates was way, way up on the scale, and the earth's magnetic field was significantly distorted. So . . ."

Dad is looking over the professor's shoulder, nodding, his dinner napkin still tucked into the collar of his blue dress shirt. "So this blast of high-energy particles cuts through the exaggerated electrical field caused by the faulty blanket controller, and bingo! No more Bobby!"

"Exactly. And of course, we don't really know how or why, and we're a long way from really understanding the interaction of the forces. But I'm almost certain we know roughly what caused it. We've got a strong electrical current field, magnetic disturbances, and an extreme particle flow. Has to be it, don't you think?"

"Has to be." Dad is nodding, and his eyes have that far-away-in-physics-land look.

Mom asks what I'm thinking: "But Leo, how can we reverse the process? How do we get things back to normal? And how do we do it before the police come to haul us away?"

Dad and Dr. Van Dorn look at each other, just for a second. And it's like they're holding this high-level, silent conference, and I see everything, and it's almost like I hear them talking back and forth: *Incredibly complex—Possibly years just to develop a workable theory—Hundreds of variables to isolate and test—Not to mention questions about body chemistry and environmental factors.* I can see this kind of stuff flashing through their minds.

Then Dad says, "Hard to say, Emily. Maybe a week, maybe longer."

And the look on Dr. Van Dorn's face says, *Maybe years.* I see it all.

I can't take it. And I'm not hungry anymore. I push my chair back and stand up. "You're not being honest, neither of you. Even if you've found the cause, really figuring it out and reversing it could take forever. And we don't have forever. I am now wanted by the law in two states, and Dad isn't going to get to do much research in jail. So tomorrow we call that lady and we get her over here, and we tell her. Then we tell the university and the people who run FermiLab, tell everybody. Show them. Then we don't have to act like criminals. Then there'll be tons of research money and facilities, and we can really figure this thing out."

Dad looks at me, at the space above my collar where he guesses my eyes are. And there's so much sadness in his face. "Bobby, Dr. Van Dorn and I discussed this situation when we spoke this afternoon. And we both decided that we do not want this to become public. Not ever. It's too dangerous. I mean, it's not like the Manhattan Project or anything, not like developing a nuclear weapon. But still, this kind of science can hurt people. Do we want invisible soldiers and police and spies all over the place? Or invisible criminals? Can you imagine the level of security we'd all have to live with if this technology becomes widely known? And even more important, do we want to sacrifice any chance for you to eventually have a normal life again? We've each promised to keep this an absolute secret, just our two families. The business with the police will go away. It has to. They can't prove anything. No motive, no crime, no evidence. Your mom and I talked, and really, all we've done wrong is lie about you going to Florida. And we can just say we did that because you'd run away, and we wanted you to have time to come home without any penalties or bad effects on your record at school. Parents can't be punished because a kid decides to run away from home. So we just have to change our story. I'm sure this is the best way. We're all sure it is."

During this speech, it's like I'm in a time machine.

All I hear is what I've been hearing for fifteen years: Everyone else has decided what's best for me. They're all sure. They've made up their minds. And now they're telling me. They're telling me how they've decided my life will be. I'm a runaway. I'm a fugitive. I'm a milk-carton kid. I'm officially missing. *They've decided.*

My jaw muscles tighten. I feel my face twist, feel my hands clench. They have such a grand plan for me.

I want to scream. I want to froth at the mouth and swear and stomp my feet and break up some chairs and throw chicken soup all over the place. And I want to yell, *It's my life! You can't leave me out of the decisions about my own life! You are not in charge here!*

But I control myself. In a calm voice I say, "I think I need to get some rest. I'll eat later."

As I leave the table, Mom looks suddenly worried, and Dad looks confused. Dr. Van Dorn seems embarrassed, so he looks down at his precious stack of data.

And I'm alone in my room. Alone. Mom and Dad are down there, spoons clinking on their bowls, ladling out soup for their uninvited dinner guest, their fellow conspirator.

And I'm alone.

chapter 26

NIGHT SHIFT

When I wake up, my alarm clock tells me it's 11:37 P.M., so from the time I lay down on my bed to now is almost four hours. All I meant to do was think a little. Instead, I've had four hours of freedom. Four hours of not being furious with my parents and Alicia's dad for trying to tell me how they've planned out the rest of my life. Four hours of not beating my brains against a wall trying to figure out what to do next. Four hours of not worrying about being this way forever. Sleep is the great escape.

Mom must have been here, because someone has taken off my shoes, and the down comforter is tucked around me. Mom and Dad looked in to make sure their little baby Bobby was all right.

My eyes are wide open. Streetlamp light sneaks around the edges of the window shades. The night-light in the bathroom paints a thin yellow stripe at the bottom of my bedroom door. The furnace blower comes on, runs about three minutes, then stops. The whole house is quiet, and I hear a bus making its last run on the street out front.

Lying still in the dark, I try to imagine that everything is normal again. I'm just a high school kid. Soon it'll be a regular Thursday morning, and I'll get up and eat breakfast and catch the bus for school. I'll doze through math, avoid speaking in French, try to look smart in English, eat lunch with Kenny and Phil, play my trumpet in the jazz band during sixth period, and after school I'll go to the library and listen to some rare Miles Davis cuts.

But I know all that's a lie. Nothing is normal.

I replay Dr. Van Dorn's visit to our dinner table. Two things stand out. First, that ACE spacecraft. It's what collects the data he found about the two dates. I've never heard of that before. I've never heard of billions of things. Truth is, I know practically nothing. Except how to take almost anything that happens and make myself feel stupid because of it. Which is what I'm doing right now.

The other thing I recall is the quick look Dr. Van Dorn and Dad passed between them. It was a secret look, the kind people exchange when what they're thinking is too terrible for words. They exchanged the look when Mom asked about reversing the process. Dr. Van Dorn doesn't believe it's possible. He thinks there's no going back. Move over, Sheila. Make some room in the lifeboat for Bobby.

Rolling off the bed, I land softly on my feet. The hallway is faintly lit, and I can tell Mom and Dad are asleep. Their turn for some freedom.

I tiptoe down the back stairs, go through the kitchen and dining room to the den. The computer sounds like a diesel truck starting up, but I know it's not really that loud.

The browser opens up, and I get to a search page, and I punch in "ACE spacecraft." And there it is, pictures and everything. ACE stands for Advanced Composition Explorer. This thing is out 1.5 million kilometers from Earth, feeding a constant stream of data to a bunch of ground tracking stations all over the world. Scientists in Japan, England, India, the U.S., they're all looking at information from ten different instruments on board. I click on the Real Time Solar Wind Data, and I'm plugged in. I've got graphs and tables and news from outer space, and the thing is updated every fifteen minutes—like the reports about traffic on the Dan Ryan Expressway.

Then I click on a link for SOHO—the Solar and Heliospheric Observatory—and it's another satellite up there in the sunlight. And there's a blinking "ALERT" on the screen next to a block of text:

The Earth's environment is currently bombarded by high-energy particles accelerated by a powerful solar eruption last night. A strong flare (M9) and coronal mass ejection were observed by the SOHO instruments. The flux of high-energy protons near Earth now is 100,000 times greater than normal. This is the fourth largest proton event in the past three years, and will likely continue at or above the current level for the next several weeks as we approach the solar maximum.

And the date on the news release is 11:45 P.M. February 24—and there's been an update every twenty-four hours right up to yesterday. The bombardment has slowed during the last month, but not by much. So what I'm reading about here on the screen, this is still going on. Now.

And it makes me smile. I wish I had a cat or something. I'd wrap it up in my magic blanket, and poof— invisible kitty. Which would be tough on the neighborhood birds.

I close the browser, open up an Instant Messenger window, and click on Alicia's screen name.

bobby7272: hey alicia--you awake?

In about thirty seconds, the program chimes back at me.

aleeshaone: hey yourself--too loud--stop til i turn down the sound . . .
aleeshaone: ok--how r u?
bobby7272: been better. how come you're still awake?
aleeshaone: duh--your message woke up my computer, and the thing starts talking to me. but i wasn't sleeping anyway. my sleep patterns are all screwy cuz it's always nighttime on planet alicia. i sleep when i'm tired. been chatting with nancy till about fifteen minutes ago.
bobby7272: bout what?
aleeshaone: you
bobby7272: what about me?
aleeshaone: none of your business

bobby7272: my imagination runs wild.

aleeshaone: that's your problem

bobby7272: so did you talk to your dad tonite?

aleeshaone: yup. said he stopped and saw you and your parents. said he's made some progress with the information, the dates--stuff about solar particles, right? so that's good.

bobby7272: is it? sounded bad to me. sounds like years of research to me. years.

aleeshaone: years don't scare me much anymore.

bobby7272: all hail the great philosopher

aleeshaone: i'm ignoring that. why so grim?

bobby7272: because i'm back where i was, only worse cuz there's no hope.

aleeshaone: no hope? how do you figure?

bobby7272: you heard your dad. he thinks maybe we know the cause, but that's not the cure. if he's right about the cause we could zap a cat or a dog or something right now. or you--wanna get invisible? i'll bring my blankie over, turn on the juice, and let er rip.

aleeshaone: --what are you talking about?

bobby7272: right now there's a big solar event-- just checked the website. big hi energy particle shower. so we grab a black lab, put him in the blanket, turn on the power, and ZAP, you could be the first blind kid on your block to have an invisible seeing eye dog! cool, huh?

aleeshaone: more like sick. how about you wrap

226

yourself up and disappear completely for a while--do us all a favor

bobby7272: naughty, naughty--don't fight sarcasm with sarcasm--two wrongs don't make a right

aleeshaone: but do three rights make a left?

bobby7272: very deep. i hear the sound of one hand clapping.

bobby7272: you still there?

bobby7272: alicia?

aleeshaone: still here. i'm thinking. two wrongs don't make a right. but two negatives make a positive, right? like in english. i'm not not going means i'm going, right?

bobby7272: . . . and your point is?

aleeshaone: in math you multiply a negative number by a negative, you get a positive, right?

bobby7272: still waiting for the point . . .

aleeshaone: go turn on the blanket and take a particle bath--you can't get more invisible--maybe it'll be like two negatives make a positive--that's the point, smarty pants!

bobby7272: right, like i'm just going to turn it on and see what happens.

aleeshaone: you're the one whining about being so hopeless. here's some hope. what do you have to lose????

aleeshaone: bobby?

aleeshaone: bobby, answer me.

bobby7272: i'll get back to you.
aleeshaone: bobby--wait. don't. i'm sorry. really, don't. something could happen.
bobby7272: you mean something bad? something worse than this? i don't think so. i'll call you in the am.

And I shut the whole thing down. The trouble with screen talking is it keeps going on and on until someone finally decides to get back to real life. And that's what I'm doing.

I walk up to the front parlor, open the French doors slowly so they won't squeak and wake up Dad. He's got my blanket carefully folded into a suit box with the controller all reassembled, set to take to the lab in the morning. Because my blanket is a scientific artifact now. I pick up the box and wind my way through the dark house again, up the back stairs and into my room.

I plug the blanket into the controller and put the controller right where it always sits on my bedside table. After I toss the feather comforter onto the floor, I spread the blanket out over the bed. Then I plug the control unit into the wall, right where it was plugged in on that Monday night. And before I have a chance to chicken out, I close my door, shut off the light, peel down to my boxers, and climb under the covers. And with my right hand, I feel around in the dark until I find the controller, then the dial, and then the little switch. But I don't flip it. I can't. Because what will happen? Will I die? Those angry words I typed down in the den, are those the last words I'll ever say to Alicia? But I have to do something. I have to. And I do. I flip it on.

A faint orange glow lights the dial, and I squint and set it to five, right in the middle, just like always. Then I lie back on my pillow and pull the covers up so only my nose is sticking out into the chilly air. Just like always. Except my mouth is dry and my chest is heaving.

And I imagine the solar wind blowing the stardust around, trillions of energized particles bombarding the earth, radiation I can't see or feel. And then I imagine I can feel the X rays and the gamma rays, feel them pinging on my eyelids, shooting through my skull, making the palms of my hands tingle like they've fallen asleep.

And I'm under my blanket, and it's warm and toasty, and my heart is thumping and my mind is racing, and I'm watching to see if the room starts to shimmer or glow.

And I feel like an idiot. Like maybe I should start chanting some magic words. Because this whole thing is so ridiculous. I'm trying to recreate something that was probably a one-in-a-billion event. I mean, it could have been a certain cloud above our house with some weird mix of pollution and chemicals in it from some power plant in Joliet. Maybe that cloud messed with the solar-wind junk before it got to me sleeping in my bed. Or Dr. Van Dorn could have just gotten the whole thing wrong. Maybe the two dates relate to some phenomenon no one has even discovered yet. Who says he and Dad know so much anyway? Their machines are big and shiny and they whir and hum, but do they really know more than some Stone Age witch doctor with a rattle and a gourd full of ground-up frog bones?

Years don't scare me much anymore. That's what Alicia just said. She's not wishing her life was different. She's dealing with the life she has. She's not trying to get back to how things used to be.

How things used to be. I don't want that. Not exactly. I'll never be exactly like I was. I just want some choices back. Even Alicia's got choices to make. Not me. I have only two. Stay hidden, or go public. And if I go public, instantly I'm a scientific oddity, front-page news. Two choices, and they both stink.

Fifteen minutes by the clock, and there's nothing. No unearthly glowing, no strange crackling sounds, no arcing electrical charges. Nothing. I feel like I should get up and go message Alicia. She probably thinks I'm turning myself into a gob of protoplasm or something. But it's 12:07 now. The digital thermostat has cut the temperature in the house back to 55. And I've been missing my good old blanket. It's too comfortable to get up and go downstairs again. Besides, that might mess up the big experiment. Right.

So I roll over onto my side and think about the things I'd like to say to Alicia. And after another five minutes or so, the sandman's got me.

chapter 27

SEARCH AND
SEIZURE

Loud voices.

It's still dark, 4:30 A.M. by my alarm clock. Loud voices. Mom's is the loudest.

"How dare you! This is outrageous!"

A man's voice, deep, and a woman's, both too soft to hear. But I know that woman. It's Ms. Pagett.

Footsteps up the front staircase. And fragments from an angry Miss Pagett: ". . . repeated warnings . . . new information . . . search is fully warranted."

Mom splutters something, and it's the man who answers. ". . . reports of lights on late at night . . . the missing boy's room."

The voices are coming down the hall, and it's the deep voice again. "This is his room."

Dad: "Are we charged with some crime? This is harassment!"

The deep voice: "Step aside, sir."

I'm out of bed now, and I've pulled off my boxers and tossed them into the open closet.

This is bad. Too many people in a small room. Someone's going to bump me or step on me. And what if someone stays in the doorway? No escape.

The door opens, and a shape fills the opening, and an arm reaches for the light switch.

I'm next to my desk, standing still. The overhead light blinds me, and I take a deep breath and hold it.

A bulky police officer comes into my room, steps quickly to the bed, and puts his hand palm down onto the mattress. He turns to Ms. Pagett in the doorway and says, "Still warm." Then he turns and looks at the papers and the cell phone on my desk, and he says, "What the! . . ."

He's looking at my desk. The list from Sears! And the cell phone—with all those numbers in its memory.

But there's nothing I can do, so I just stand still. He comes toward the desk, right toward me, and I'm ready to duck and roll, maybe get under the bed. And he looks me right in the eyes and says, "Who are you?"

I stand stock-still.

He's still looking into my eyes. "I said, who are you?"

Ms. Pagett is in the doorway. She's looking at me too. And behind her, Mom and Dad.

I look down, and there I am. My body. Me.

"I—I'm Bobby Phillips." And I'm naked, and I grab up a sweatshirt from the floor and use it to cover up. And I'm dazed, and I must look like an idiot because I can't stop grinning.

Ms. Pagett has turned to face my mom, furious. "What is going on here!"

Mom knows she has to say something to Ms. Pagett, but she keeps looking past her to smile at me. Then she focuses, takes a deep breath, and says, "What's going on? You want to know what's going on? You've just burst into my home and terrified my son, that's what.

He got home from Florida late last night after a long train ride, and the last thing he expected was to have armed storm troopers crashing into his room at four in the morning!"

"Well . . . why wasn't I notified of his return?" Ms. Pagett is still trying to sound tough, but she's already retreating, and Mom is on the attack.

"Why?" Mom takes a step toward Ms. Pagett, and the lady flinches. Mom's voice is shrill. "Why weren't you *notified*? Because this problem you've been trying to solve has never been any of your business, that's why. There's never been a real problem. You've tried to make our family's activities into the state's business, and you assumed Bobby was lost or missing or who-knows-what. But we have never been uncertain about his safety or his whereabouts for one moment. And did you expect me to call you at home last night so you could meet him at the train for us?"

Ms. Pagett doesn't know what to say. "We were only able to work with the information we had—"

"And we appreciate that." Dad's turn. "We know that you've been doing your job, and by your standards you had reasonable cause for concern. And when my wife has had the rest of her sleep, I'm sure she'll be less angry than she is at the moment. Now, is there anything else we can do for you?" Then, turning to the cop, Dad says, "Officer, is there something else you need to search for?"

The cop looks at Ms. Pagett, and he's embarrassed. He says, "No. I think that does it, right?"

Ms. Pagett nods. Mom steps back, and Dad moves

aside, and the policeman and Ms. Pagett walk out of my room, down the stairs, and out of our house.

Here's the summary of what happens next: hugs, kisses, some tears, some hot chocolate, more hugs, and a lot of talk. First, I explain about the ACE and the SOHO websites, then about messaging Alicia and her double-negative idea. And then how I just got the blanket, plugged it in, and got into bed. I don't tell them how my last thoughts were about Alicia.

Dad almost flips out because he's never performed a big experiment without thinking about it for at least a year or two. The physicist is angry about me taking this step with "such an incomplete assessment of the variables and the risk factors." But the father is proud about me being so bold. And both the physicist and the father are blown away with the results.

But as I talk with Dad, I can see the wheels spinning in his head, and I know that the scientist is just itching to take that blanket and try it out on something else— maybe a little white mouse.

Mom won't let go of my hand. We're downstairs on the couch in the living room, and she keeps reaching over to push my hair up off my forehead. My hair's a lot longer than it was a month ago. And she keeps tilting her head and smiling this goofy smile at me. I feel like her eyes are devouring my face.

But you can only take so much of this kind of stuff, and after about half an hour, I start yawning. And Mom can see me yawn. She can see I look tired. And she can see me smile when she says I ought to go back to bed.

And Dad says, "But *not* under that blanket—please!"

And we all laugh, and that sets off another round of hugs.

Mom comes upstairs with me. She takes the blanket off my bed, folds it carefully, and puts it on my desk chair. Then she picks the comforter up off the floor, spreads it over me, and tucks me in. And she bends down, runs a hand through my hair, and gives me a kiss on the cheek. And I'm glad.

Alone in the darkness before dawn, though, I can't sleep. Much too excited.

Today will be Thursday. I could get up at 6:45, shower, eat at 7:15, catch the bus at 7:37, go to school, and have a regular day. Regular Bobby having a regular day.

But I don't think that's going to happen. There's some other stuff I need to take care of.

chapter 28
LOOKING AGAIN

It's about 9:00 A.M., and I spend at least five minutes in front of the mirror after my shower. Which is about ten times more time than I ever spent back then, back before. For a month there was nothing to see. It's like I have to remember how I look again.

Mom doesn't want to go teach her ten o'clock class. She wants to stay home and moon around, find some more excuses to sit and look at me. She wants to fix me another breakfast, maybe go with me to the barbershop. She wants to be the new, improved Mom. Which is actually quite nice.

But I don't want to go the barbershop. I like my hair this long. Maybe even longer. It looks good. Only time will tell. Time. Now I have time for things like growing my hair.

When Mom finally leaves at the very last second, I'm glad. I've got stuff I've been waiting to do.

The first thing is to call Sheila. She answers on the third ring.

"Sheila? This is Bobby Phillips. We talked about your blanket a couple days ago?"

"Hi, kid. How's it going?"

"I'm back."

"No!"

"Really. And it was so simple. I promised I'd let you know, so . . . I'm letting you know."

"And it was simple?"

"Easy as falling asleep. But I think you might have to go north. And you have to wait for the right conditions. I made some notes for you, about how it works. Should I mail them, or send you an e-mail?"

There's a pause. Then she says, "Did you keep your promise? About not telling about me?"

"I only told Alicia, the girl I told you about. My dad wanted to talk to you himself, but I didn't tell him."

"Good. Now I have something else I need to ask you to do for me, okay?"

"What?"

"Forget you ever found me. Forget my name. Forget we ever talked. Don't tell anyone about me, don't ever call me again."

"What about—"

"Don't tell me anything else. I've been thinking about this ever since you called."

"But—"

"Listen. Don't talk, just listen. I've thought about this a lot. And what I figured out is, I started disappearing a long time before this happened to me. If it hadn't been this, I would have disappeared some other way. Booze or drugs maybe, maybe three more bad boyfriends—that would have done it. I was already disappearing, a little bit at a time. It was better happening all at once. And now I don't want to go back. I don't want to start worrying about my weight and my hair and all that junk again. I like who I am, and I've got a life that works fine. It's fine for me. So I'm going with it."

I don't say anything.

She says, "You don't understand that, do you?"

"I think I do."

"It's just as well if you don't. Listen, kid, I'm happy for you. Really. I hope it all works out the way you want it to. So take care, okay?"

"Okay. So long. And you can call me anytime, if you want to."

But she's already hung up. She's gone. And I put the phone down.

Sheila thinks I don't understand her. But I do. That's the thing. I do understand. Because a week ago, back when there was no hope of a comeback, I didn't have any responsibilities. None. I was a floater. A week ago it was all about living, just living, minute by minute. No tomorrow, no future. No tracks. No expectations. Not really here. Mostly gone. And there's a kind of freedom in that. And I wonder if I'll miss it.

And now that I know how it's done, would I do it again someday, on purpose? So I could take a vacation from life?

And what about my dad and Dr. Van Dorn? Are they going to be able to let it lie? Or are they going to team up and try to win the Nobel Prize in physics one day? Publish their findings on the Internet? Where's it really going to end?

Sheila's already decided where it ends. It ends with her. She's made a life that she likes. She's like the guy who spends sixteen years in jail, and then gets out, and hates having to make all the decisions of regular life. So he steals a car or something to get himself sent back inside. Back where it's warm and dry, where you already know about all the dangers, where you don't have to make any decisions.

Sheila likes her prison. It won't surprise me if she moves to a new town in a week or so. She'll probably change the name of her business, cover her tracks. I'm not her rescuer. I'm a threat.

Sometime I'll sit down and try to figure out why I'm not like Sheila. But not today. Too much to do.

I don't take the bus to Alicia's house. It's a long way, but the sun is out, it's in the mid-fifties, and I am wearing a shirt, some jeans, a jacket, Nikes—everything. It's a great day.

I walk past school, and I think maybe I should go in and say hi to the nurse. I could do some push-ups for her, let her know I'm fine, tell her that I'll be back in school soon. Or maybe not. Maybe I really will take the rest of the semester off. Might make me graduate late, might even set me back a whole year. So what? Years don't scare me much anymore.

I made Mom and Dad promise not to call Alicia's parents. I wanted to tell Alicia myself, in person. And the closer I get to her house, the more nervous I feel. Because things are different now. And how do I talk to the person who just gave me back my life?

Mrs. Van Dorn answers the door and looks at me, her eyebrows up. "Yes?" she says.

I guess I thought maybe she'd be able to recognize me, like maybe some weird sort of intuition would kick in and she'd give me this big smile and say, "Wait—you *must* be Bobby!"

It's not happening. She has no idea who I am.

"Mrs. Van Dorn, I'm Bobby Phillips."

Her mouth drops open, and her eyes bug out, and she says, "Oh! My goodness, you're . . . you're here! Bobby, I'm so happy for you—and for your parents! This is wonderful! Of course, I feel like I know you, but it's very nice to . . . to see you this way. Please, come in, come in!"

And I know that what she really likes best is that she doesn't have to imagine me walking in her front door naked anymore. And she's glad that I don't look like some complete Neanderthal with my knuckles dragging on the ground. Mrs. Van Dorn is into looks, and now she can relax because she knows what her daughter's friend looks like. In my head I'm getting ready to launch into a lecture about appearance versus reality, but I hear Alicia call, "Who is it, Mom?"

And her mom calls back, "It's for you, Alicia," and she smiles a scrunchy smile at me and whispers, "I'll be in the kitchen." Because now that she knows what I look like, it's safe to leave me alone with her daughter.

Then Alicia's at the top of the stairs. She's wearing the green sweater and red corduroy pants she wore that first day I talked to her in the listening room. Her head's tilted, her hair falling away from her cheek. She's trying to pick up on what's happening. "Hello?"

Using a neutral tone of voice, I say, "Hi, Alicia."

She's coming down now, stepping surely, right hand on the railing, her face a flurry of emotions. "I was so worried about you last night." Then accusingly, "And it was just mean the way you signed off. I was going to call you, but it was almost midnight." She's stopped about two feet from me in the entry hall. Her face brightens, and she says, "But I'm glad you're all right— everything is okay, right?"

"Yeah," I say, "fine. Except for one thing."

Her face clouds over again, genuine worry. About me. And I feel like a jerk for playing things up this way. So, real fast, I say, "But it's a good thing—because now I have to wear clothes out in public again. You were right last night—two negatives make a positive!"

Alicia doesn't get it for a second, and when she does, for another second she doesn't believe it, and then I can see she knows I wouldn't kid about that, and she lights up with this huge smile. "You *rat*! Really?! You did it, with the blanket? And you . . . and it worked?"

And she's coming toward me, reaching out, and I stand still and meet her hands with mine, and she feels my jacket sleeves, then quickly up the arms to my shoulder and neck, feels my collar, and then runs a hand down my shirtfront to my belt. It's a clothes check, to make sure I'm really wearing them.

And then she brings her hands up again, this time toward my face. And she gets a shy smile on her face and says, "I have to do this, okay?" I guide one of her hands to my cheek, and she feels me nod as I say, "Okay."

Her fingers are light and cool, and I close my eyes just for a second. An involuntary shiver runs down my spine as her fingers trace across my forehead to touch my hair, and then back down across my brow. Her thumbs meet on the bridge of my nose, and I feel like a book being read, word by word. Eyebrows, lashes, cheekbones, nose, lips, chin, jawbone—the oddest ten seconds of my whole life. And watching her face as she takes her mental tour . . . I'd like to be touching her face too. I watch her and try to imagine her seeing me, watch her try to match up this new physical image with what she already knows.

She lowers her hands, and she's blushing, the spell broken. Then she says, "Come on!" and grabs me by the hand and pulls me toward the family room. "Tell me everything!"

She's the best audience. It's so much fun to see her face as she pictures everything I describe. And when she can't believe something, I have to tell it again and add more and more details until she's convinced it happened. Like with the cop searching my room at 4:30 A.M.

"No way!" she says. "This guy's looking right at you, and you don't know it? How could you not know it?"

"Because a month of being invisible makes you feel that way, that's how come. And then he's right in front of me looking me in the eyes. That's the first time someone's looked me in the eyes for a month. And that's when I knew."

"Didn't you die, like, standing there with nothing on, and everyone looking at you?"

"Well, yeah, and I grabbed a shirt and held it in front of me—but really, I was just so blown away. Really. Like, feeling embarrassed was way down the list. And then you should have heard my mom start spinning out this story about how I just got back last night. It was crazy."

When I tell her about my call to Sheila and what she said to me, Alicia nods slowly, and her eyes get shiny. Her eyes still work fine for crying. "That's so sad, don't you think? I mean, giving up that way? But I know how she feels. And it is her life."

"Yeah. That's what got me so mad last night—your dad and my parents, saying how they'd decided everything for me. They didn't have the right. Just like we can't tell Sheila what to do."

Alicia nods. "Right. But you can't help feeling like you should sometimes. The way Sheila's story makes me feel?" She drops her voice to a whisper and points toward the noises her mom is making in the kitchen. "It's probably the way my mom feels about me—like she has to butt in and try to help all the time."

And then neither of us knows what to say. But the silence isn't strained. We're both comfortable, just sitting here on the couch, not touching, but close. I look at her left hand. It's resting on the dull red corduroy of her pants, palm up, long fingers slightly bent. And all her fingernails are chewed down to the quick. I've never noticed that before. And without thinking, I reach down and take her hand and lift it up so I can see it better, feeling the tip of her index finger with my thumb.

"You almost chewed this whole finger off."

She's turned toward me on the couch, and I'm looking into her face, and it's hard to believe eyes this pretty don't work. And I'm feeling like I want to kiss her. Which is not the first time I've felt this way, but without a body, with just a shadow-body, it never felt right before. It was one of those things I couldn't see myself doing.

I'm starting to lean down toward her face when suddenly she pulls her hand back and turns away. Tears again.

I ask, "What is it?"

She swipes at her eyes with her sleeve, and shakes her head.

"Must be something."

"Duh!" she snaps. And then mocking, " 'Must be something.' Brilliant, Bobby, brilliant. In fact, I think I'll call you Brilliant Bobby—how's that?"

She stands up, tosses her head, feels her way to the end of the couch, gets her bearings, and then stalks out. I hear her footsteps across the tile in the entry hall, and then she stomps up the front stairs. A distant door slams shut.

Jeez.

Mrs. Van Dorn comes into the family room. My face must tell her everything. I'm out of practice. For a month I haven't had to hide what I'm feeling.

She comes over and puts her hand on my arm. "Don't take it personally, Bobby. She gets mad at almost anything. Maybe give her a call this afternoon, okay?"

And she walks me to the front door, and she tells me again how happy she is for me and how great it is that everything's okay now.

But as I start walking home, everything's not okay now. All I can think about are those little fingernails, chewed down to nothing.

Back home I go into the den, turn on the computer, and open up Instant Messenger. I click around to see if Alicia's online. She is.

bobby7272: hi alicia. it's me.

Nothing. And I try about six more greetings. Nothing. So I just leave it on and hurry down to the basement to find a cardboard box. Because walking home, I decided to do something. Something only I can do. I grab a box and run up the stairs to my room because I have to do this fast, like, maybe it's already too late. Because maybe it's gone. The blanket. Because I didn't actually see it this morning. Maybe Dad took it to the lab.

But he didn't. It's folded up on the seat of my desk chair, right where Mom put it early this morning.

So, I put the blanket and the controller into the box. I grab the sheet with Sheila's address and stuff it into the back pocket of my jeans. I put the list of names from Sears into the box, and I pick up the cell phone and clear its memory.

I take the box, trot down to the parlor, scoop up all Dad's notes and diagrams plus the information sheets about the electric blanket, and toss them into the box.

Back in the den I check the messenger window. No response yet from Alicia. I open up the browser, find the SOHO page I looked at last night, and then print out a copy and toss it into the box.

In the kitchen I rummage around for almost ten minutes, but I can't find any strong tape. But I do find a black Magic Marker, and I put that into my jacket pocket.

Three blocks away, I hurry up the front steps of the post office. At a table I write Sheila's name and address on the box. Then I wait in line with the box.

The man in the blue shirt has a big mustache.

"Regular delivery or express on this?"

"Um, surface is okay."

"Parcel post will cost . . . three dollars and ten cents. That'll take about a week, maybe more. Or you can send it priority. Be there in two days, but it'll cost you . . . six dollars and seventy-five cents."

"Priority, please. And can you close it up with some of that tape?"

"Sure."

As he reaches for the tape, I say, "Hey—can I put one more thing in there?"

"Yup, but you'll have to get back in line."

I take the box back to the table, and on the blank side of an insurance form I write,

Sheila—
I wanted you to have this stuff, just in case.
Bobby

I'm not telling Sheila what to do. I just want her to know that anytime the sun acts up, she has a choice.

Five minutes later, the box is in the hands of the postal service.

When I get home, there's a message waiting for me on the computer screen, very short.

aleeshaone: check your email

I do, and a letter is waiting.

dear bobby,

sorry im such a mess. face it. im a mess. im never going to be fun to be around. ive been kidding myself into thinking we were such friends. more than friends. you were like me. thats how it was. you had a problem, i had a problem. i could even help you. i dont get to help much. everyone helps me. and part of me wanted you to never get back. to need me. not now. now youre back. back to school and friends and girls and prom and college and everything. youre back and im not.

i was online with nancy when you kept trying to
message me this morning. i told her about you, about
everything. i dont think she believes it all, but she
believes youre real. she asked me if you ever kissed
me. i said almost.

the last time i kissed a boy was 8th grade. tommy
seavers. kid stuff.

you almost kissed me today. i felt you. so close.
but it would have killed me. because i dont know if i
can see that. i cant see us. i can see you, but i still
need to see me. and i feel like you see me. do you?
you do. you almost kissed me. so close. with you its
not kid stuff.

i wrote a poem. not about that. about everything.

basement room

i think its raining from my basement room.
but basements make for faraway ears,
and rain dries up so quickly.
i still think it was rain.

i think a wind is blowing up above.
but wind is such a meaningless thing,
invisible and always gone.
i still think it was wind.

i think im up there in the wind and rain.
but dreaming is always done in bed,
and so many winds and rains are dreams.
i still think it was me.

like it? nancy thinks its good, and my mom the lit major says she doesnt really get it, and my dad hasnt had time to read it. figures. hope you like it.

see that? how i hope you like it? im just sure you are going on. going away from me. off into the big bright world. a whole life thats not near mine. hurts.

and then today. so close. and it felt like maybe you werent going away. like you came to see me. to see me. and that was scary too.

there are mirrors in my house. i remember them. i still touch them. smooth and cold. i used to look. all the time. people do that. not just me. its true. store windows. little mirrors in cars. makeup mirrors. anything that reflects. and not just girls. everybody. all the time. to remember what they look like. to make sure they dont disappear. like maybe theyre already gone.

i was almost gone bobby. i was almost all the way disappeared. i couldnt remember if i was real. i

couldnt see who could love me. i couldnt see anything
there to love. i couldnt find a reflection. anywhere. i
needed a mirror so bad.

and that was you bobby. invisible mirror. i see me. i
see you.

love alicia

People talk about crying from happiness, and it
sounds stupid—crying from happiness. I never knew
what it meant. It's not really happiness that makes the
tears. It's everything at once, everything that's good and
sad and wonderful all at once, except the things that are
wonderful mean so much more than the sad things.
Crying from happiness, right there, sitting in front of
the computer, reading Alicia's e-mail.

I wipe my eyes on the sleeve of my jacket, and I start
to open up Instant Messenger. Then I stop, and I print
out Alicia's e-mail, and then I shut the computer down.

I fold up the letter and stick it in my pocket. As I open
the front door, something moves. I turn, startled. It's
me, in the big hall mirror. But I don't stop to look. I'm
out the door. I'm in a hurry. I've got to get over to
Alicia's house. I need to tell her how much I love . . .
how much I love her poem.

And I need to be there to see her face when I tell her.

THINGS NOT SEEN
Discussion Guide

1. What would you do if you woke up one morning to find that you were invisible? What do you think the hardest thing about being invisible would be? Would you behave differently if no one could see you?

2. What if you had the ability to change yourself in one big way? Would you become invisible, fly, have superstrength, etc.? What would you do with your new talent?

3. This is a fictional story, but people can feel invisible in real life when they are ignored or shunned by society. Can you think of other times in history when an individual or a group of people have been treated as "invisible"? Have you ever felt as though you were "invisible"? What did you do?

4. As humans, we know that we will be seen by others. It is a fundamental truth, or a fact of life. What is another fundamental truth—something that you take for granted? How might your life be different if that changed?

5. What do you think of Bobby's relationship with Alicia? Do you think they would have become friends if he had not become invisible or if she had not been blind? How do you think the story would be different if one or both of them had not been changed by the situations in their lives?

6. Bobby and Sheila have very different ways of handling their problems. Which way do you think was better? What would you have done if you were in their situation?

7. What do you think is the most important thing Bobby learns about himself during his adventure in invisibility?

Turn the page for a Q & A with
ANDREW CLEMENTS

A Conversation with Andrew Clements

Where do you get your ideas for books?

Most of my story ideas come from my own life in one way or another. If I'm writing about school, I remember the years I spent as a student myself, the years I spent as a teacher, the years I have spent as a parent of children in school. And I dig around. It's like being a miner. I dig around in this huge pile of memories, find a little chunk of an idea, and I work on it and polish it up, refine it into something useful or interesting.

How did you come up with the idea for *Things Not Seen*?

Invisibility is not a new idea—it's actually as old as God. And books about people who become invisible—that's not a new idea either, but most of these earlier books were either science fiction or scary, mad-scientist stories. I just wanted to explore what might happen if a normal kid woke up invisible one day. Would it be pure fun, or would there be another side to the experience? And that idea got the story started.

Are any of your characters similar to you? Did you ever do any of the things they do?

When I was a fourth-grade teacher and kids would come up to me and ask, "Mr. Clements, how do you spell 'pancakes'?" and I would say, "Go look it up in the dictionary!"—Mrs. Granger in *Frindle* says that a lot. So in a way, Mrs. Granger is sort of like me. Yes, there are little bits of me in all of my characters.

What was your favorite book as a child?

When I was very young it was the Winnie-the-Pooh books by A. A. Milne and *The Little Fireman* by Margaret Wise Brown. Later, I loved *The Call of the Wild* by Jack London, *Kidnapped* and *Treasure Island* by Robert Louis Stevenson, the Sherlock Holmes mysteries—all sorts of books. I read a lot.

When did you know you wanted to be a writer?

I knew I loved reading and books early on, but didn't realize I was a good writer until a high-school English teacher named Mrs. Rappell made me work at it. Once I'd figured out I was a pretty good writer, I went through years and years when I wrote short things—mostly poems, descriptive sketches, song lyrics. I wrote short things because I didn't make the time to write and because writing for me is not easy—which is true for most people, and which is especially true for most writers. I taught school for years and was good at that; I worked as an editor for years and was reasonably good at that, too. Knowing

I wanted to be a writer was not a lightning-bolt moment. I simply discovered over many years that writing is what I seem to do best.

If writing is not easy for you, why do you do it?

On a windy, drizzly fall day in New England, I stacked firewood for five hours straight, three cords of wood—it had to be a couple tons of the stuff. It was difficult, but come winter, there would be a cheery fire in the fireplace, and toasty warmth from the stove in my writing shed in the backyard. I like cheery fires and toasty stoves enough to want to do the hard work of stacking wood.

I know from my own experience that reading a good book can be a life-changing event. So I'm willing, actually happy, to do the work of stacking all those words so they'll give off some heat and light in another's life on a winter afternoon or a summer night. And if I have the ability to perhaps make that happen, then the work becomes fun.

Where do you write?

Most of the time I write in a little shed in my backyard. It's small, only ten feet wide and twelve feet long. It's about seventy feet from the back of the house, and it's quiet out there. There's no phone, no e-mail, no TV, no music system. There's a door and two small windows. There's an air conditioner for the summer and a woodstove for the winter. There's a three-feet-by-six-feet plank-top desk, a comfortable desk chair, and the laptop computer I carry back and forth. And there's also a folding cot that my wife and kids gave me for Father's Day. And that's it.

With whom do you share your writing first?

My wife, Rebecca, is my first and best critic. After she's read it, it goes to my kids. When work is ready to leave the house, it goes to my agent and the project editor, sometimes one before the other, sometimes simultaneously.

Do you read reviews of your own work?

Yes. It's hard not to. You learn to be grateful for the good ones. You learn to be tolerant of the ones that completely miss the point. You learn to resist the temptation to fire off an indignant e-mail. When reviewers write, I nod politely. I hear what they have to say. But when librarians and teachers and parents tell me what they think, I listen. And when kids tell me what they think, I really listen.

Do you have any advice for aspiring authors?

First rule: Read, read, read. Read all the good books you can to learn what good writing sounds like and feels like. And think about what you read. Remember that everything you read in a book happens on purpose. Try to figure out why the author chose that particular word at that spot in the story—because he or she did choose that very one and not all the other possible words. Then, you have to write yourself. And find good teachers to help. Read books about writing. Read what authors say about their own writing. And above all, be persistent.

What's the best question a reader has ever asked you about your writing?

A boy once asked me, "Aren't you afraid you're going to run out of things to write about?" I thought about that one carefully. But the answer has to be no. One of my greatest discoveries has been that there is no shortage of good ideas.

Discover the rest of Bobby's story in the gripping sequels!

★ "Clements hits no false notes in this beguiling sequel . . . Not since *Frindle* has Clements's writing achieved such near perfect pitch."　　　　　—*Publishers Weekly*, starred review

★ "A riveting story line, engaging characters, and intriguing insights into the development of musical artistry."
　　　　　　　　　　　　　　　　　—*Booklist*, starred review